MURDER
BY SCHEDULE

by

JULIAN HINCKLEY

With Illustrations By
Paul H. H. Stone

Foreword

Early in 1937, a detailed account of Martin Field's sensational "perfect murder" was first presented to the reading public in narrative form. In view of the recent revelation that an outstanding hero of World War II—South Africa's famed Wing Commander Archibald Meadows—was none other than Martin Field; and in view of the distorted and falsely-colored versions of that "perfect murder" appearing in recent months in newspapers and magazines, it has been thought desirable to publish anew, in revised and more closely-authenticated form, Julian Hinckley's absorbing and springtly account of one of the most fantastic cases in criminal annals.

Hinckley has had the willing cooperation of his rediscovered friend Field himself in clearing up certain doubtful points that existed in the initial version of that shadowy adventure—an adventure the stigma of which has now been so gloriously expiated in gallant service to the cause of decency.

We believe the reader will be as amused and astonished as were we to find how long ago and far away now seem the ante bellum nineteen-thirties, in whose other-world atmosphere—caught with such skillful indirection by the author—this breathtaking and ingenious story unfolds.

—W. N. J.

CHAPTER 1

THREATS!

'Damn you, Mortimer, I intend to choke Creighton Fortescue
with this letter!'

A QUIET afternoon at the club. October 3rd, six p. m. A bit
late for tea; a bit early for cocktails. The late sun streaming
in through the high velours-curtained windows made solid blocks
of light out of the smoky air.

There was the usual representation present. Always, of course,
there was the old colonel in his favorite deep leather chair by the
window, from which he had appraised the run of feminine beauty
on the Avenue for almost fifteen years. His silvery white locks
belied the thoughts that went on in that old, but not too reverend
head.

Then, too, there were the backgammon and contract regulars,
their games over, their anæmic energies spent, their post-mortems
finished. A couple of young Wall Street members had sunk them-
selves deep down in the financial pages of the evening papers.

A very pall of quietude, indeed.

It was such that young Freddy van Leer, pausing for an instant
on the threshold, remarked upon it to his white-haired companion,
Peter Townsend, "My heavens, not in there!"

4

"You're a young man looking for excitement, adventure, romance, aren't you? A bit of pall, and you funk. Well, my boy, the consular service isn't all *hula-hula*. You'll find many a tropical island post that will make this room seem like a night club in full swing by comparison. You will eat lotuses for a time, till you take to eating your heart out, and then for want of some one to talk to your mind will turn in on itself. And that does stranges things to a man: it develops mysterious and not quite holy faculties."

"Let's go up to the bar."

But something in the silence of that big, dim room with its bars of sunlight, like the sunlight beating through the heavy growth of the dark jungle, something in that stillness, seemed to hold Townsend. He stood there in the portal sucking his empty pipe, his clipped white mustache bristling under his high-beaked nose as he sniffed.

"Hm-m-m!" he said. "It's quiet enough for almost anything to happen."

"Oh, come on," said Van Leer impatiently.

"No. Just one moment. This quiet—I remember once in Sumatra ——— Funny, you know, the uncanny instincts that one acquires in the East. You always know when something is going to happen out there—a native uprising—the first cases of plague. There is a silence like held breath; the ominous silence that pervades everything just before an earthquake—a sort of expectancy. Funny, you know, after all these years, but——— Suppose we stop in here a minute."

Very quietly, Townsend moved into the room, found a pair of deep leather chairs in a corner near the door, and took out his tobacco pouch.

"Besides, there was something I was meaning to ask you about these heads. Shall we sit here?"

As Freddy reluctantly gave way and flung himself into one of the chairs, Townsend went on in his slightly Oxford-accented voice.

"About these heads, or should I say trophies of the chase?" He pointed to the collection of stuffed heads that filled every available space of the four high-paneled walls. "Martin Field recently presented them to the club. He is a friend of yours, isn't he?"

Van Leer's face brightened instantly.

"Oh, yes! He's told me a lot about places—East Africa and the like. Gosh, but he's a wonderful fellow! He's the finest man I ever met. Honestly! He's got everything. Take that last expedition of his—when he got all these heads—what sport!"

"Sport?" Townsend's inflection was questioning. "There's something I never could quite understand."

"What don't you understand?"

"The pleasure, or the satisfaction, or just what is it that any one can get out of killing these wild things."

"You don't! My gosh, man, what wouldn't I have given to have been on that expedition! What wouldn't I give to go anywhere with Martin Field!"

"Would you, really? I suppose it's the killing instinct—something I've missed. Probably the fault of a Baptist upbringing. Ah, speak of the devil and who should turn up but Field himself."

Van Leer sprang up. "Hello, Martin. Come, join us."

Martin Field had been standing quietly in the doorway for some seconds, surveying the occupants of the room with a rather grim contempt.

Field was a tall, thin man just turning forty, with a handsome bronze mask of a face beneath prematurely graying hair. A striking figure of a man, as he stood there so straight and yet with such an air of relaxed ease. There was something level and compelling in the glance of his gray eyes under that fine forehead, and something, too, in the glint of white teeth as he smiled that grim smile.

Field's level glance took in Van Leer and immediately dismissed him, then straying to Townsend, the glance flashed an instant acknowledgment of the latter's presence. Here was some one worthy of his notice. He moved toward the two men.

"Hi, Martin!" cried Van Leer again. "Townsend has got some queer bug about sport. Just tell him how you got that rhino, will you? I'd like him to know what it feels like to get a rhino."

"Do," said Townsend, touching the stem of his pipe to his forehead in a sort of military salute. "I should like to hear it. I was remarking on your quite extraordinary collection of heads."

Martin smiled his fine smile. "Well, to be frank with you, Peter, I didn't know what the hell to do with them. They make the place look rather like a zoo. What's your impression?"

"My first impression, if you must ask," replied Townsend, "was that we'd enlarged the membership. But you don't mean to tell me you went all the way to Africa to shoot these wild things without knowing what for?"

The friendly smile died instantly on Martin Field's bronze mask. "You must meet an old aunt of mine. You and she would enjoy discussing cruelty to dumb animals." He rose from his chair.

"Oh, now, really, my dear fellow, you've misunderstood me,"

said Townsend. "I'm not at all a sentimentalist. You see I have been, in my own small way, a hunter myself."

"I see." Martin Field's tone was dry, suspicious. "And what was your game?"

"Men," replied Townsend, knocking the ashes out of his pipe. "You know, of course, that for years I was in the Secret Service. I hunted spies—dangerous game."

"You did?" Martin slowly resumed his seat. "Go on about that. I'm interested. Interested——"

"Oh, well, this killing of wild animals as a sport is something that I've missed—unfortunately. But perhaps not quite altogether. There was a tiger that had got three of my coolies. I hunted him in such a rage that I didn't sleep for five nights. Not till I'd got him. I remember kicking the dead thing in the face. Did you feel that way when you brought down that rhino? It must be a great satisfaction."

Martin Field did not reply. He sat staring. It was Van Leer who broke the spell with his easy, boyish laugh.

"What a damned crazy idea of sport! I suppose a fellow would have to work himself up into a rage to shoot clay pigeons."

"Shut up a moment," said Field, not too politely. "I wish Townsend would say that all over again—in exactly those same words. No, I suppose you couldn't, and you needn't. I get the idea. And the men you hunted——"

"Spies. Naturally, in wartime one's animosities——"

"Animosity. Hate."

"Yes, but there's another side to it, too," continued Townsend. "It's what I should call the sporting side. My young friend here said that it was preposterous that a fellow should have to lose his temper in order to shoot clay pigeons. Well, I'll go him one better. I'll have it that the clay pigeons must turn on him in a blind rage. I meant by that——"

"I see perfectly what you mean," said Martin. "To a man who has hunted such dangerous game as spies, these trophies must seem like so many clay targets."

"Come, now, I said nothing of the kind."

"Ah, but it's the truth. It's what I've had in the back of my mind for years. I love animals. But what else is there to hunt? The War's over. Gunmen—— Yes, I suppose I could get our fellow member, District Attorney Mortimer, to swear me in as a special detective. But I doubt if that dumb ass would appreciate my services."

"Better not talk so loud," said Townsend. "It's very quiet in here."

Even as he spoke, they were all aware of a stir at the far end of the room. Some one with an open newspaper clutched in his hand was approaching them. It was District Attorney Mortimer himself. Seeing him, Townsend shot a grim smile at Van Leer.

"My Malay instinct," he said under his breath.

Martin Field looked up from his preoccupation into the face of the man he had just called a dumb ass.

"I have been listening," began Mortimer succinctly. "And I am glad that Martin Field can take this attitude about this zoo of his, because I, for one, am strongly in favor of having all these damned heads thrown out of here."

Silence fell for an instant after this outburst. Martin Field got slowly to his feet.

"Why, you—you———"

"*Dumb ass* was your latest epithet," interposed Mortimer.

Martin nodded as one bereft of speech. "Right," he said. "And no apologies, Mortimer."

"Come, gentlemen," interrupted Townsend diplomatically. "I'm afraid I started this. It's my fault."

"No, you didn't," said Martin speaking with great deliberation. "It is a matter of many years standing between us."

The district attorney smiled. "He is referring to a little affair of breach of promise. You didn't do so well under cross-examination, Field, if I remember rightly. Those letters of yours—speaking as you gentlemen were, of trophies—take those letters now, especially the one beginning———"

"Gentlemen! Gentlemen!"

"Or if trophies are to be valued for their decorative effect, it is a pity you ever turned from women to dumb animals Field. Those earlier proofs of your sporting blood—even that Miss Sussman would have made a decorative panel. Though, to be perfectly frank with you, I never thought she quite merited the ardent admiration you expressed for her in those letters. Well, good evening, gentlemen."

But Martin stepped suddenly between him and the door. His manner was restrained, smiling.

"I owe an apology to these slain beasts," he said. "Townsend is right. I had no animosity against them, and there was no satisfaction to me in killing them. There's only one trophy now that will give me any real satisfaction."

"You are referring to my scalp, no doubt," replied Mortimer. "You're just a few years late getting that, I'm afraid." He laughed as he touched his bald spot.

"You're not that decorative, Mortimer, that the club would ever want you stuffed. And as for intelligence—well, as a dangerous adversary you probably overrate yourself."

"We must share the same weakness," returned Mortimer. "Shall I leave you the evening paper?"

The tone of this offering brought another pause.

"I take it that there is something in it that applies to me," said Field.

"It must be a small matter, indeed, that would not touch you somewhere—a man of your size."

Martin snatched the paper from the district attorney, and with a justifiable vanity turned to the headlines on the front page.

It was there, of course, in big print.

NATIONAL & TRANSATLANTIC CO. IN RECEIVERSHIP.

For a moment the black letters seemed to come alive like snakes. He drew his hand across his eyes.

"Receivership——" He laughed. "Why that's impossible—quite impossible, with Fortescue back of the company. Creighton Fortescue couldn't let me down like this. I've a letter from him here in my pocket." He fumbled for it. "He says the Holland International hasn't sold a share. There's two hundred millions back of the company. I've Fortescue's own word for it. He got me to take over ten thousand shares from the Wharton estate. That was not two weeks ago." Field paused, seeing the look in Mortimer's face. "Oh, so that was it? Swindled!"

"Of course, it's only a small matter to you, Field—ten thousand shares—otherwise I shouldn't have drawn your attention to it," said Mortimer with evident pleasure.

A flood of righteous rage possessed Martin Field.

"Why, the filthy vermin! A man like that isn't fit to live. Look at this letter telling me——"

"Really," interrupted Mortimer, "I suggest that you have it framed and present it to the club. I'll make a speech for you." Then suddenly he threw back his head and laughed.

There was no longer silence in the big room. Martin Field, standing there under the glittering glass eyes of his slain beasts, was aware of an echo of Mortimer's laughter coming back to him from other parts of the room. Never in all his life of adventure had he so felt the challenge of a situation. Mortimer had him down, shoulders to the mat.

But Martin Field had a power within himself that he had always relied on in moments of necessity or peril. Something demaniacal inside of him took hold of the situation.

"Exactly," he said. "As a matter of modesty, I should appreciate your making the presentation, Mortimer. I am quite sure that, presented by you, the club members will find it an acceptable trophy. Because, damn you, Mortimer, I intend to choke Creighton Fortescue with this letter. That, I believe, is as near as I can actually come to putting Fortescue's head up on these walls."

Townsend stood up.

"Gentlemen, I feel that we have all been talking rather absurdly."

"Why, not at all," said Field. "This is just what I've been looking for. You had your spies, Townsend, but the War's over. Now, I've got Fortescue, and I don't have to go all the way to British East Africa after him. He lives two floors below me on Fifty-seventh Street. To complete the bag, I've Mortimer, here, a rare specimen of the equine family. I shall bring him back to you as a new species, distinguishable by the bray."

"You're talking rather big even for you, aren't you?" asked Mortimer.

"I have those ten thousand shares of N. T. C., still worth something, to put up against any odds you may suggest, Mortimer. What about that little matter of framing and presenting this letter? You will make a nice speech of presentation in your best courtroom manner. What do you say?"

"Are you insane? I think I'll be going."

A man driven by a fatal ambition, coupled with a taste for the limelight, Mortimer was acutely sensitive of ridicule, much as he endeavored not to show it.

As he went out into the street he was wishing he had left Martin Field alone. The man must be crazy! To have taken him seriously was even more grotesquely ridiculous. He felt very much let down in his precious dignity.

Meanwhile, Martin Field had sunk himself into Van Leer's vacated chair and barricaded himself behind Mortimer's newspaper.

A low buzz of voices now filled the room. Townsend emptied his pipe, drew a deep breath as one who acknowledges a certain fulfillment, rose, touched the dumbfounded Van Leer on the shoulder.

"There, my lad, that's that. Now we might as well go on wherever you say. Funny, you know—always just before the storm a peculiar quiet. In Java once—or was it Sumatra—"

And his voice with its Oxford intonation died out down the hall to the club entrance.

CHAPTER 2

THOUGHTS IN THE NIGHT

For twelve years Martin had lived with savages, a law unto himself.

THE whole affair had been brief and to the point. Although there had been a dozen or more witnesses to it there was but one version, a categorical sequence beginning with Peter Townsend's challenge to Martin Field's sportsmanship, followed by Martin's inadvertent reference to the D. A. as "that dumb ass," and Mortimer's return thrust with the newspaper headlines. Then there had been Martin Field cooly betting Mortimer ten thousand shares of National & Transatlantic that he, Martin, would kill Creighton Fortescue—would choke him with his own letter—ten thousand shares against a speech of presentation by the D. A. when the letter, having served its grim purpose, would be properly framed and, in lieu of Fortescue's head, be hung among the African trophies on the club walls.

Up to this point one uniform version. But thereafter the greatest diversity. Variously recalled, Martin had been smiling and self-possessed, and Martin had been in a blind insensate rage. He had known and meant what he said, and had no idea what he was saying. Or perhaps it was just a Gargantuan jest involving as it did, ten thousand shares of a stock worth anywhere from nothing to half a million. Those who insisted that Martin was not to be taken seriously were haunted by the look that had been in Martin's eye as he had made his bet, while those who advocated Martin's immediate arrest did so a bit sheepishly as if fearing that the laugh might be on them.

Of course, Creighton Fortescue must be warned. But who in this exclusive gentlemen's club knew the fellow personally? Fortescue, the plunger, a *Lochinvar* out of the West, the outlaw in a silk hat. He ran a brokerage office for racketeers. A familiar figure about the night clubs, but to phone him—there was no member of the club present who cared to claim that degree of intimacy. The proposition became another loose end of argument.

They had all seen Martin go out of the room. They had followed his movement as far as the cloakroom where he had collected his hat and coat. But no one had seen him actually leave the club.

In fact Martin had left by the rear basement entrance. He had paused amid the refuse barrels in the narrow alley that led from the kitchen to the street front. It was quite dark. He waited until the pupils of his eyes had expanded and then moved cautiously to where the alley was opened on the street. He paused here.

On the opposite side of the street a yellow taxi waited, a space of open curb on either side of it. Martin edged into the shadow and felt in his overcoat pocket for a small pair of opera glasses. With these he raised the opposite facade of the street, bringing them to a final focus upon the yellow taxi. He had not to wait long. Some one in the taxi struck a match. A cigarette was lighted —two cigarettes. A light was passed forward to the driver. Nor was the driver alone in the front seat. Thugs——

A slight shiver passed down Martin's spine. He cast his mind back over the last few hours in which he had unconsciously outwitted Fortescue. Fortunately he had flown back from the game at Princeton. More fortunately he had not gone to his rooms directly above Fortescue's. A lucky break that. Fortescue must have counted upon it. For, of course, there was only one way in which such a swindle as that in National & Transatlantic could have been put over. Society would have thought nothing of his, Martin Field's, disappearance—another hunting trip, no doubt. But Fortescue had missed getting him by one edition of the evening papers.

Up to that point blind luck had saved him. But from there on, Martin had reason to congratulate himself on his training in the bush, on his quickness of perception of danger, his trained nerves and his presence of mind. In this first opportunity to apply his intelligence in the opposite role of the hunted animal he had known enough to attack before being cornered.

This he had done instantly and without hesitation by publicly announcing that he would add Fortescue's head, so to speak, to his other trophies. He emphasized his serious intention by backing it with a bet of half a million. Now if Fortescue got him first, Fortescue would instantly be apprehended for it.

Unless, of course, Mortimer——

But just where did Mortimer stand with this banker-racketeer?

Martin waited in the dark of the alleyway counting the minutes on his pulse. Ten—fifteen——

At last! Another yellow taxi stopping beside the one across the street. A signal; then both cars pulling out and away into the traffic.

Martin stepped quickly out into the lighted street and looked at his watch. Twelve and a half minutes.

So, that was how long it had taken Mortimer to reach Fortescue; that was how close the D. A. stood in with the racketeer.

A rare thrill of apprehension passed through Martin Field. The jungle was safer, he thought. And his heart, as always, yearned for the forest where for the better part of the last twelve years he had lived with savages, dispensing his own justice to his *safari*, a law unto himself. It was for him to revert to the point of view of a civilized man in a highly organized society. He knew its law, having once studied it, but his feeling was for primitive justice.

Well, here he was in for it now. He must get his enemy before his enemy got him. And above all else he must do it alone. He despised the law. But still he would commit no one else to his lawless enterprise. He had made his bet to get Fortescue, and he would get him without benefit of gunmen or the law's hangman. His sporting soul stood up within him. Here at last was his ultimate quarry.

Half an hour later Martin was in his own plane, flying to his private shooting preserve on the northern watershed above the headwaters of the Saguenay River in Canada. His route lay from the flying field south of Jersey City up the Hudson River to Albany, with here a fifty-mile hop to Lake George and so on over Lake Champlain to the St. Lawrence. It was perfectly safe even at night for the small amphibian cabin plane.

An expert flyer, with a somewhat uneventful War record, he seldom now took the controls himself, preferring to let his mechanician act as pilot.

Chuck, the mechanician, was a young Canadian guide whom Field had taught. Plane-struck, the boy had attached himself to Martin three years before up in the woods. He had become Martin's guide, his shadow, his mechanician, his pilot, always with that infinite resourcefulness of one born in the woods and brought up to fend for himself under pioneer conditions.

He had no false pride about taking any orders that Martin gave him. And he did take orders. In the early days of teaching Chuck to fly, Martin had taken him up to the plane's ceiling and had then put his nerve and ability to take orders to the test by making him loop and barrel-roll till he himself was dizzy.

Chuck had come through the ordeal and could now flip the plane with the same native-born knack with which he flipped Martin's flapjacks over the camp fire.

Martin sat now behind Chuck, watching him, considering the chances. Eight hours to camp; eight hours in which anything might happen to the plane. There could be no coming down or stopping over. Everything must be certain that the boy would make it. Not this flight, but when the time came.

Martin took out his watch and checked the time. Seven-fifteen. The Hudson lay silver beneath them.

Chances—— Of course, there were chances. Without chances there would be no sport. Clay pigeons! Which of them had said that? Oh, yes, Van Leer! Yes, he'd said it, but he hadn't meant it that way. Van Leer was on his side.

Yes, Van Leer would do nicely. He fitted almost too perfectly into his plan. The boy's family, what there was of it, lived abroad. Freddy was waiting for a consular appointment, and would probably have to wait several months yet. That could be easily seen to. Then, too, he lived at the club. He was not tied up with any girl who would question his absence, or a possible broken date. And the boy had only one thought in his young head: shooting and fishing.

Yes, Van Leer would do. He was Heaven-sent. It was a cinch.

But, the radio! The radio had almost been forgotten. Suppose he had forgotten that! Of course, the one at camp could easily be put out of commission. But suppose the boy was one of those radio fans that built their own sets and was expert enough to repair it? Then, too, there would be other sets in the near-by lumber camps. He would have to clear them all out of there. Every camp, every hunting party—positively no trespassing. He would enforce first of all a rigid prohibition of radio sets among the guides.

No chances! No chances!

Planning—he would allow himself all of two weeks for that. There was plenty to think out, but one could do a lot of thinking in the uninterrupted silence and seclusion of the woods.

Martin Field congratulated himself on having the most secluded and inaccessible preserve in all Quebec Province. A vast tract, it was where a man could get away from that civilization that he had never felt that he quite understood. In the southern part of it one might meet an occasional mining prospector in summer, and in the northern part there were a few half-breed trappers working for the Hudson Bay Company in winter. One found their camps, and frequently their bones, in the spring.

It was just the place to send Van Leer. Even if the boy wanted to leave before it was time, there would be a way to hold him without his realizing that he was being held. Chuck could manage anything as easy as that. Get Freddy snowed up, or, as a last resource, have him kidnapped and held for ransom. Chuck was wonderful when it came to what he called "putting on." He would get lost or play sick. A perfect program of such devices would have to be planned and ready. No chances! It might be necessary to plan for three months—four months, while he himself would be locked up. Everything must be done in advance. No chances! To plan for every possible contingency—— Gad, what an undertaking!

And so he sat planning while the plane roared on through the night.

CHAPTER 3

PLANS

One had only to look into Fortesque & Co. to know what sort of man Fortesque was.

IT was typical of Martin Field that he never thought about what other people might be thinking of him. His singleness of purpose was not embarrassed by any consideration of what interpretation might be put upon his sudden flight from town. Possibly it was being said that he had fled to save his face; but what of it? Indeed, what did it matter what they said? Except, of course, that he depended on its being repeated to Fortescue.

It was Martin's way of throwing down the gantlet. The swindler would know that he was fair game. Martin took that for granted and it was all that mattered. He would flush his bird before he shot.

Field was right in this. For if the affair at the club did not actually reach the newspapers it was, at least, all over town by noon the next day. Nothing else was spoken of downtown. The N. T. C. receivership became the veriest side issue.

And what had happened to Field? Of course, he had run away. Of course, he was hiding his face.

The telephone rang and rang in the apartment as the curious tried to get Martin on the phone. There was hardly an office in Wall Street that didn't think up some pretext for calling him up.

Van Leer, in his ingenuous loyalty to Martin, not to say his importune youth, went so far as to call personally at Fifty-seventh Street. He had once dropped Martin off there, though Martin had not pressed him to come. Something of a hermit Martin was, or, perhaps, being rich, he was cautious about encouraging hangers-on.

Van Leer had no difficulty in finding the place. It was one of those private apartment hotels with one main entrance and separate private entrances, each serving a limited number of apartments.

Freddy tried the private door and found it locked. He rang the bell; waited. He rang again. And again he waited. Presently a small colored boy in uniform appeared in the main entrance.

"You looking for some one?" he inquired.

"Yes, I'm looking for Mr. Field—Mr. Martin Field. I'm Mr. van Leer."

"I reckon Mr. Field must be gone away. He most is," said the boy.

"Oh, has he, really? Could you tell me how long he is to be away?"

"No, sir. But you can write him care of the Bank of Manhattan, downtown. He has an office in the building. It's way up in the top."

"Yes, I know. Well, thanks."

He called Martin's office, but got no answer. That, too, was a luxury. An office with a key that you could turn in the lock when you stepped off for Canada, Africa, or the South Seas.

He even peered in at Creighton Fortescue's brokerage office and caught a glimpse of Fortescue himself.

Obviously, Fortescue was keeping discreetly in the background, offering no explanation and inviting no questions on the matter of his deal with Field. Of course, he could hardly have taken Martin Field's threat to choke him with his own letter seriously. It could only have been constructed as a bit of imaginative pleasantry.

Certainly Fortescue was no lily-livered milksop. A hard-bitten, sleek, not to say slick-looking man in his middle forties, the New York representative of one of the biggest Chicago produce exchange firms—no one quite knew what his origin was or where he had served his apprenticeship, and Van Leer felt very callow in his company.

One had only to look into the customers' room at Fortescue
& Co., to know what sort of man Fortescue was. For here were
the big plungers and the black sheep, the fellows who sat up
all night in poker games, the bootleggers and bookmakers, flashy-
looking gentlemen from the West come East on nobody's business
but their own.

And always a representation of women, old women with lifted
faces and pouchy eyes, and girls from the revues, the very pick
of the chorus, also about their own business. Even the stenographers were different, and bore out Fortescue's reputation as
being a connoisseur of women—on the physical side.

Something of distinction could be claimed by having the same
tailor as Fortescue, who affected a certain dandyism with his top
hat and cut-away coat that was betrayed into commonness by the
diamond ring on his finger. There was always a slight aroma of
alcohol about him. On his desk in his private office was always
a half empty highball glass. He had a nervous habit of shuffling
a pack of cards while he talked to any one. Not that he had
ever talked to Van Leer. He simply looked straight through him.

Certainly Creighton Fortescue was not a man to be afraid of
Martin Field. And yet Van Leer observed two men in that customers' room who obviously did not belong there. Detectives—

A week later when he stopped in again there was only one
detective, and he, too, presently disappeared. Nobody spoke any
more of the affair at the club. Martin had gone off and would
probably never dare show his face in New York again. Van Leer
saw Fortescue at the Downtown Club going about as usual.

Yes, the excitement had all blown over. It left a sort of vacancy.

Van Leer, waiting idly for his consular appointment, was feeling extremely bored with the stock market, the club, week-end
parties and life in general when he got Martin's telephone call.

"Good heavens, is that you, Martin?"

"Yes; I've been up in the woods."

"Any luck?"

"Well, no—I wasn't shooting. Lots of game, though. Wish
you'd been there."

"Wish I had. Only you didn't make the suggestion."

"Didn't I? What about that appointment?"

"Not a word."

"What are you doing?"

"Twirling my thumbs."

There was a brief pause. Then Martin said, "The place is lousy with game. I must have counted two dozen moose. And one old fellow must have had a spread of eighty inches."

"Did you get a shot at him?"

"I'm not shooting. That is one reason why I called you up. The other reason is a white black bear."

"A white black bear?"

"Sounds silly."

"You mean an albino."

"Of course. Winter coat, too. But something seems to have got into me. I let him go."

"Why the hell did you do that?"

"Don't know. Just couldn't feel any of the old thrill. But there's no reason for being a dog-in-the-manger. How would you like to go after him?"

"Would I? Wow! When?"

"Are you quite free? I don't suppose you have many social engagements at this season."

"Not a date."

"Sure?"

"Absolutely. I'm all set for my sailing papers from the State Department."

"Fine. I'm sending the boy right back with the plane. Are you ready to go at once?"

"You mean right off the bat? Why, I don't know. I suppose so."

"There's just one thing, though. You know I'm taking a big chance calling you up. If anybody ever found out I was in town — Well, anyway, I figured on your discretion. But it's got to be more than that. *You've got to follow my schedule to the second.*"

"I understand. You can depend on me."

Martin's voice made a low, sharp sound in the receiver.

"Here's the plan, then. My watch says five thirty-two. I may be slow. Can you be at the corner of Fifty-fifth and Sixth Avenue at, say, five forty-seven? You'll have to drop everything and run to make it."

"Right-o!" shouted Van Leer and slammed the receiver on the hook. He had only time as he grabbed his coat and hat from the boy in the check room to gasp, "Off on a trip and don't know when I'll be back."

CHAPTER 4
ACTION!

He hardly heard the shot himself above the terrific bang of the door.

MARTIN FIELD also acted quickly, but with such precision of movement that his actions seemed deliberate and unhurried. He had called Van Leer from his own rooms. Now as the receiver clicked, he, too, hung up, and taking the .32-caliber Colt revolver from the drawer of his desk, went out into the elevator hall.

The elevator was there with the door propped open. He had only to step into it, push the button, and swiftly descend two floors. Again he left the elevator door open, thereby assuring himself that the car would remain at this floor, because the motive power did not function when the door was open.

He stood for the merest moment listening, experiencing again that thrill he had not felt since his first shooting trip. He had listened then to the padding of hooves through brush, but now he listened to the sound of two colored comedians on the radio in the apartment on the floor below, a faint clicking of a typewriter on the other side of Fortescue's door and the rush of running water.

Had Fortescue been a wild beast, Martin would have noted certain habits peculiar to the species. It took hot baths at five thirty p. m. It used the typewriter for its correspondence of an actionable nature. Click—pause—click, click. A laborious evasion of breach of promise. Click—pause—click—pause. It sounded like a meditative woodpecker. From the street outside came the sound of traffic, the siren of a passing fire engine, the back-firing of a truck. A good moment—*to do murder!*

All set! Martin Field touched the butt of the revolver under his left arm beneath his coat. Ready, on your mark, get set. Steady now. Steady. He knocked.

Oh, damn! It could not have been worse. A bad, suspicious-sounding knock. He had probably scared away his bird.

He listened. The clicking had ceased.

With trembling hand he knocked again with a light feminine rap and continued a gay drumming with the tip of his kid-gloved fingers. It was a long, long time since any woman had knocked on Martin's door, but how well he remembered the sound!

Still Fortescue was on guard. "Who the hell's that?"

Martin tried the door, but found it locked. He renewed his drumming, tapping out now a silly rhythm.

"Well, who is it?"

Martin played the coy visitor. He did not answer. He ceased tapping and made a scratching sound with a glove button.

"I won't open the door till you say who you are. Oh, I know; it's you, Margot."

Martin scratched again, this time furiously with both buttons.

This seemed to reassure Fortescue, for after a moment he came and unlocked the door. At the sound of the key turning in the lock, Martin quickly thrust the door open and found himself face to face with Fortescue, who was holding a small, nickel-plated revolver.

Martin had quite expected this. He laughed. "Strike me pink, if here isn't more of it! Say, old man, what the hell's all this about my having you stuffed, you ugly brute? I've been away for weeks."

He paused. It was strangely like whistling in a bird to a blind.

"What has Mortimer been up to—one of his little jokes?"

"Jokes?" repeated Fortescue, staring stupidly as the sudden significance of the idea dawned upon him. "Do you mean to tell me some damned fool's been making fun of me—that you didn't—— Where've you been?"

"Up in the woods. Just got back this morning. Found everybody laughing."

"Laughing? Oh, they are, are they? Laughing!"

And the silly bird set his wings for the decoys. Rather quickly, and shamefacedly, Fortescue lowered the little nickeled revolver and put it behind him.

"Everybody is laughing. But what's it all about?" said Martin taking one step inside the room. "I'll close the door."

Well rehearsed, he had his lines and action perfect. As he turned now putting out his left hand to the doorknob he reached his right hand up under his coat. Then with all his strength he slammed the door.

He hardly heard the shot himself above the terrific bang of the door. As Fortescue fell forward with the revolver pressed against his chest, Martin caught and eased him to the floor. There was no sound of a falling body; just a rattling of last breath, and then, once more, the roar of running water in the bathroom and —comforting sound—the voices of those colored comedians on the radio in the room below.

First Martin locked the door and put his revolver in his pocket. Then he shifted Fortescue's body to a small bearskin rug.

Kneeling, he felt in the dead man's waistcoat pocket, found there the bunch of keys he sought, crossed the room to a flush-paneled door with a cylinder lock.

He had tried three of the keys before he found the right one. The door being opened there was revealed a miniature bar, and it took but a minute to drag the bearskin with Fortescue's body upon it into this hiding place, to close and lock the door.

He placed Fortescue's little revolver on the desk. Then he shut off the running water in the bathroom, turned out all the lights, listened a second at the hall door, opened it, fixed the latch to lock upon closing, went out into the hall and closed the door behind him. He had only to step into the elevator and he was back again in his own room.

He now looked at his watch. Exactly three and three quarters minutes had elapsed since Van Leer had rung off.

Although Field had all the time he needed—twelve minutes— he was breathing hard as four minutes later he pushed through the doors of a telephone pay station on Broadway. He gave the switchboard girl the club number and was presently assigned to a booth.

He lifted the receiver and almost immediately heard the desk clerk at the club say, "Hello."

Martin said, "I vant to spik to ze menager."

"I think you must have the wrong number."

"Ya? Vat number you got?"

He strung the call out for nearly a minute and a half before he asked to speak to Rosie and the man at the club rang off. Then he went back to the switchboard.

"Get your call all right?" the operator asked patting her curls. There was nobody else in the place.

"Yes, thank you," replied Martin. "Do you suppose that clock of yours is right? It seems slow to me."

"You said it! Slow? You're telling me! I'm off at six o'clock, though."

Martin smiled his most destructive smile. "Sorry I can't take advantage of that information. But I've got another date—to meet a gentleman on the corner of Fifty-fifth Street and Sixth Avenue at 5:47. I just made it this minute with you listening in."

"Aw, no, I don't never listen in!"

"My watch must be damn near ten minutes slow. I meant to set it when I came by the Pennsylvania Station just now."

"Wait a minute—I'll give you the time. Hello! Meridian 7-1212."

They waited.

"Fifteen seconds past 5:45. There you are."

Martin set his watch. "Nine minutes slow. This will make me late for that appointment—except, of course, we compared watches. So he'll be just as late as I will, won't he?"

As he went out he felt confident that she would remember. This silly little mustache, however, was just enough to prevent her from recognizing his photograph and coming on before her cue. That would be fatal.

Ffffui! How any one could want to wear a mustache! Whiskers had a natural use in keeping the face from freezing, but what good was a mustache except to strain your coffee? He was not sure that the best part of a shooting trip was not the feel of the razor again when one got back to civilization. Well, now that he had bagged Fortescue, he would shave this remnant of his backwoods virility. *Ffffui!*

He did not have to hurry. He meant to be a minute or two late. He wanted to be dead certain that Van Leer would be there ahead of him, would be watching for him, and would see him coming from the direction of Broadway.

CHAPTER 5

ALIBI—AND FLIGHT!

Martin knew instantly that Fortescue's body had been found.

LADY LUCK, though fickle toward many, was stringing along with Martin Field so far. Martin saw that Freddy van Leer was running true to form, for there he was—hopping up and down in his boyish impatience on the southeast corner. Good grief, the boy was wearing spats!

Van Leer described Martin from afar.

Perfect! Martin came on briskly now, signaling to Van Leer to remain on his side of the avenue, waiting that long minute and thirty-eight seconds of the crosstown red traffic light.

"Hi, Fred! Sorry to have been so precise about your getting here on time, but that was part of my escape. That's the trouble with women—if they just didn't hang on! If they would only learn to weep quietly and not cling! Hope you didn't mind being rushed. There really isn't any hurry, unless you want to do some shopping. Sports' Shop will be closed before we can get there. I know a very good little sporting goods shop on the West Side. How do you like my Gable mustache? Got a cigarette? Here's the car on the other side of the street. How are you, young feller? Feeling fit? On your toes?"

"Yeppee, and rarin' to go! Say this is swell of you, Martin. Tell me about that albino black bear."

The light of hero worship shone in the boy's blue eyes. Wonderful to be like Martin, to have everything in life and to use it, too. And especially wonderful to be able to have affairs with women and not be ashamed, to be able to come from an affair with that urbanity that could treat of women and big game in the same breath!

He covered these thoughts quickly. "And what about that moose, too? The eighty-inch spread?"

"That's the one I'd go after if I were you," said Martin. "You can use my license. I never pulled a trigger the whole time I was up there. The guide has got it. His name, by the way, is Chuck. You call him Chuck. He flies the plane, too. A marvel at it. This is the car."

If Van Leer had expected an expensive imported model he was disappointed, for it was a perfectly commonplace black eight-cylinder sedan, so undistinguished in the company of the other cars parked along the curb that Martin had to look twice to identify it.

They got in and Martin took the wheel. As they pulled out into traffic, Martin asked:

"Well, now, what about equipment?"

"It's all out in the country," said the boy, his face lengthening. "I haven't been out hunting for over a year. It's all up in the attic. I've done a little skeet shooting on week-ends and some revolver target practice up at the squadron."

"I used to be pretty good with a revolver, myself, in my romantic youth. That was before the Sullivan Law. The only use I've ever had for a pack of cards was to shoot the spots off them at ten paces. I've a ten of clubs somewhere with ten straight hits. But to get down to brass tacks—what about equipment? You'll need something besides spats. Look at you!"

"You didn't give me time."

Martin laughed. "That's all right. I've got every sort of togs up there. I keep extra ones for guests. What size shoes do you wear?"

"Nines."

"Same here. You'll have the choice of six pairs."

"I hate to borrow your things, Martin," objected Van Leer.

"I have the same fastidious feeling about that, myself," said Martin. "Wearing other people's clothes. But I think there are a lot of new things—guest outfits, flannel shirts, corduroy pants, lumber-jack coats, sweaters, shoepacks. And I keep a box of cheap handkerchiefs. If you want to dress for dinner every night——"

"No, no! But are you sure you want me to borrow all your things? I feel rather——"

"Nonsense. That's what they are there for," insisted Martin. "I'll lend you a couple of hundred dollars cash if you think you'd like it, though there's nothing to spend money on. You'll be back here before you'll have the chance to spend a nickel. We're on our way—at least you are. Wish I could be going along with you. Perfectly lovely up there. No snow yet, but, boy, was it cold last night!"

"This is getting more and more exciting!" cried young Van Leer. "Just where is it?"

"Do you know where the Saguenay is? Well, it's a big stretch north of the divide with practically nothing between you and the Hudson Bay. Chuck will put you down on Mistassini and you work in from there. I've got two good men who'll look after you. Yes, they'll take good care of you, because I don't want anything to happen to you."

"What's going to happen to me?" laughed the boy.

"Nothing," replied Martin rather shortly. "I've seen to that—unless you shoot yourself, or break your fool neck, or get lost. What about appendicitis?"

"Had it out when I was at school."

"That's one chance that's out." Martin's tone of voice had changed subtly. "I'm having Chuck look after you. I've given him rather strict orders. Of course, he will take your orders, too."

"Don't worry about me. I'll wear my rubbers and say my prayers. What's the matter with you, Martin?"

"I'm taking no chances," returned Martin so shortly this time that Van Leer held his own tongue for a space of ten blocks.

They had been crawling westward in traffic and now turned south on Eleventh Avenue, proceeding at a fair rate of speed.

"Where are we going now?" asked Van Leer, breaking in on Martin's mood.

"Holland Tunnel."

"So we're really on our way—just like this?"

"Why not?"

"But, gosh, man, if you don't mind, I've got to telephone——"

"Not a chance."

"Or at least drop a note."

"Not a chance."

"Why not?"

"Not on my schedule."

"Oh, I'd forgotten that," said Van Leer apologetically. He flushed then, remembering that what he had really forgotten was Martin's crazy act at the club two weeks before. No wonder Martin was driving fast and furiously. No wonder he wore those silly little lines of hair under his nose. It was damned nice of Martin to have taken all this trouble and risk of being recognized just to give him a chance to get that bear.

"It doesn't matter," he said quickly. "Thing is, I'm waiting for a letter from the State Department. Suppose it comes while I'm away."

"I'll take care of it. Where would you like it to be sent? What about Sumatra, where everything is so quiet just before something happens?"

Van Leer laughed. "Say, Martin, you were wise to have ducked out. You had the whole town unbuttoned for a week, and Wall Street with its pants down."

Here they plunged into the tunnel and further conversation ceased while they roared through that place of echoing white tiles.

Martin concentrated his attention on driving, and Van Leer had an opportunity to glance sidewise at him. It was easy to see that Martin had something on his mind. There was a fire in his eye and the muscles beneath that lean brown jaw worked. Van Leer thought to himself how glad he was that he was not in Fortescue's shoes, for all that Fortescue had for the moment the upper hand of Martin. Any one who properly admired Martin Field would have to be a little afraid of him.

Emerging from the tunnel, they proceeded through the most crowded part of Jersey City. Quite suddenly Martin pulled in at the curb in front of a small drug store flanked by a kosher butcher shop and a pawnshop.

"Here's where you can get your toothbrush," said Martin, "and anything else you may need."

"I won't be a minute," replied Van Leer, "and I won't give you away by telephoning. It was damned nice of you to run the gantlet to give me this chance in the woods."

"Thanks," said Martin.

But he watched the boy closely through the lighted window. And no sooner had Van Leer returned than Martin seemed to have a sudden idea.

"Look. Isn't that a Colt in that pawnshop window? The one

just under that violin hanging up. If it's a Police Positive .32 I'd like you to take it up with you. I used to have one, but I seem to have lost it. There's no Sullivan Law over here, you know. Ask how much he wants for it."

"You stay here," said Van Leer.

In less than two minutes he was back in the car. "Got it. Eight bucks, including one box of shells."

"Let me see it. Yes, that's the gun. In what sort of shape is it?" Martin was pulling out into traffic again.

"Good enough," replied Van Leer, examining the weapon closely. "A little rusty here on the trigger guard. And somebody must have been using it to drive nails. Look."

Martin searched in his upper waistcoat pocket.

"I've got a nail file here somewhere. Ah, here it is. See if this will take the rust off."

Van Leer took the nail file. "That only makes it worse. Takes all the blue off. See—scratches it. Guess I'd better not fuss with it."

Martin made no reply, but there was that glint in his eye again.

Now they turned off down a side street, into a labyrinth of alleys. Away from the bright lights of the shops and the street, darkness suddenly closed in round them.

Martin drove slowly, silent and intent on some business of his own. Twice he paused by the curb only to drive on again without explanation. Presently they came to a crowded water front —the Hackensack River. Again Martin pulled in at the curb and stopped the car.

"Wait here," he said shortly.

There were no street lights here. No lights of any kind. The very buildings reflected darkness. Martin found a passage between two coal pockets, groping along a dirty wall in the direction of the river. He emerged upon a sort of wharf with a crane and a great pile of crushed rock. He could smell the river, but he could not see it.

He felt his way farther in the dark and came at last to a line of sheet piling under which lay a cluster of scows. Beyond these the river glistened black and oily. There was nobody about. He listened intently for a moment and then, taking the revolver with which he had killed Fortescue from his pocket, he dropped it between the ends of two scows into the dirty water.

"Perfectly simple!" he said to himself.

Indeed, everything so far was exactly according to schedule.

Fortescue was dead and the weapon that had killed him was disposed of. This dark access to the river, the drug store and pawnshop with its police service revolver in the window had all been part of his plan. He had spotted them all that morning.

Luck had attended him, especially in having found Fortescue alone in his rooms. But Martin knew the species, knew its habits, knew that its Saturday nights were sacred and that a relaxed hour or two of anticipation and privacy were an essential part of the rite. He had expected to play the role of *Charlotte Corday* to Fortescue in his bath. He had waited for Fortescue to come in, and the sound of that running bath had been his cue. No great amount of luck about it; just knowledge.

Luck, perhaps to have reached Van Leer on the telephone so opportunely. The boy might have been out of town on a week-end, which would have meant putting the whole business off a week, or even two weeks. Luck certainly, but certainly not the sort of luck that left much to chance.

Something in the finality of the thing made him pause. He had killed Fortescue, but that was the least part of it. He had now to get away with it. Not so easy to get away with murder. Just to drop the incriminating weapon in the river was not enough.

Martin wondered what his chances would be at this stage. Suppose he hopped on his plane with Van Leer and flew back to Canada? How long would it be before Fortescue was found? How many persons had seen him, Martin, coming and going? How would he make out under cross-examination? And there was that open assertion of his at the club that he would kill Fortescue.

These reflections did not, however, interrupt the order of his movements. He lost no time in groping his way back through the dark alley to the street. He emerged hurriedly from the dark passageway without looking in front of him and he had even taken several steps toward his car before he noticed the policeman standing beside it.

For an instant then he was in utmost peril. Something he had read of but had not been able to imagine and so prepare for, took possession of him—an impulse or an instinct to cut and run for it. As it was, he stopped suddenly. What saved him from running he did not know, unless it was that his feet had become lead. For several seconds he could not move at all, and in that moment he recovered control of himself. And that demoniac presence of mind of his told him what to do.

Enacting the characteristic buttoning gesture of a man who has just performed an act of nature he went forward. Without paying any attention to the policeman he walked around to the street side of the car and got in. The policeman, satisfied, moved on.

But Martin had driven almost ten blocks before he heard Van Leer talking. What the boy had been saying Martin had no idea, but Van Leer was suddenly becoming insistent.

"Look here, Martin, I would like to know."

"Know what? Wait and see. Everything is all fixed. I'm sorry I wasn't exactly listening. I've been thinking about something important. The plane's at the Jersey City airport. But a new idea has come to me. There's no hurry. Suppose we stop here and have a drink."

"Swell," agreed Van Leer. "I need one. What sort of a joint is this?"

"Looks like old times," laughed Martin. "A real old corner saloon of the gay '90s."

"Amusing," said Van Leer, hesitating between his desire to show himself a man and a natural fastidiousness. "But, Martin——"

"Oh, it's never so bad after the first drink—if it hasn't knockout drops in it," replied Martin. "If you'd drunk in some of the places I've crooked the elbow——"

"I bet you have."

They locked the car and went in. A disillusioned-looking bartender rose from behind the tabloid newspaper to receive them. Martin ordered a couple of martinis and commented on the emptiness of the saloon.

"Not much to show for Saturday night."

"Naw."

"What's the matter? Aren't people drinking since prohibition?"

The bartender shook his bald head. "They go to the damn movies."

"So the damn movies have saved mankind after all!"

"Or else they take the wife and the kids out in the car," added the bartender. "The young folks they got teams and the ones ain't got teams they got goils. All dancing and jazz. Goils—" His tone was particularly sour on that syllable of contempt. "Drink it out."

"Have one with us," said Martin.

"T'anks."

"To the gay '90s when naughty was naughty," proposed Van Leer, lifting his glass. "To the Demon Rum."

The bartender wiped his mustache, that badge of an ancient

trade, on the back of his hand. "Naughty? Why, nobody thinks about drink like that no more. That's what's wrong with it. It ain't wrong no more. Wicked? What, to these times? Just a slap on the wrist. If you want to be naughty these days you start with murder and go on from there. Seen the latest?" And he reached behind him for the tabloid.

Martin knew instantly that Fortescue's body had been found. He knew also that the police were after him and that the airports were all being watched. Mortimer would not spare himself. The motor-cycle squad would be out on every motor highway.

"Let's go," he said. He felt in his pocket for the money to pay for the drinks and his fingers encountered Fortescue's keys.

He saw Van Leer reach for the paper, saw the bland unconcern on his callow face, saw the headlines—the word MURDER—GIRL MURDERED—show girl—possible suicide.

He took out his handkerchief and wiped his mouth.

"Phew! Say, Mike, you want to wash out the bathtub before you make up the next batch of that gin. Come along, Van. We're on our way."

They stopped next at a roadhouse capable of providing entertainment for upward of five hundred guests at one time. A vast sign in electric lights proclaimed "DANCING." Through the stained-glass windows of its porch enclosures, came the thin sound of a full orchestra—by radio.

They went in. The place was quite empty. They had the idle choice of a hundred tables. A shabby waiter handed them a mimeographed menu. It was obvious that yesterday's baked meats would coldly furnish to-morrow's feast. Nothing could have been more dismal than that vast place.

They ordered dinner and waited. The regular dinner they discovered later—much later—had to be cooked in its entirety, except for the watery soup that committed the guest to his contract.

Meanwhile the radio provided entertainment with the echoing, throaty blare of music heard in a vault, interrupted now and then by the announcer cautioning them against the perils of sour stomach and sluggish bowels, and abjuring them to "buy a box tonight."

It was all exactly as Martin had planned.

"I've been figuring it out," he said suddenly. "It takes eight hours flying to get up there. But I've been thinking that it won't do for you to get there before sunup. I told you it was cold last night. Suppose the lake's frozen? Chuck might have trouble finding a landing. As soon as it's light he can pick a patch of open water. That means hanging around a bit, because you can't take off before ten o'clock."

"Oh, gosh, if I'd known that——"

"I know. It was stupid of me. But I am glad I happened to think of it at all. And I suppose you won't mind wearing my flying togs. There was something else, too. Oh, yes! You'll use my 403. It's the finest rifle you ever sighted. Had it specially built. Sights flat at four hundred yards."

"Swell!" cried Van Leer. "But have we got to wait here till ten o'clock?"

Martin smiled inscrutably. If Van Leer was finding it trying having to wait till ten o'clock, how would he feel if he were in Martin's shoes? Just to sit at this table and wait for so many hours to drag by—and with Fortescue's body hidden in that closet! This was by far the hardest part of it. But he concealed his thoughts. "If there's one thing there's no sport in killing it's time," he said.

"I bet it's a *rara avis* for you, Martin. So you've quit killing wild animals, have you? Because of what old Townsend said, I suppose."

"I sort of forget that he said anything," said Martin. "When and what?"

"Why, at the club that afternoon that——"

"That what?"

"The afternoon you said you were going to get Fortescue," said Van Leer, embarrassed.

Martin wrinkled his forehead. "Just what did I say?"

"Why, don't you remember?"

"Was it anything so important?"

"Only that you said you were going to shoot Creighton Fortescue and have him stuffed, or something like that."

Martin laughed. "Yes, I remember. And why isn't that a good idea?" And he added, "I'd rather be killing Fortescue than killing time like this, wouldn't you?"

Van Leer forced a laugh. "But look here, Martin, you've put yourself in a bad spot. You can't say you're going to kill a man and——"

"And not kill him? You mean that Fortescue will hold it against me if I don't?"

"I mean that you made yourself—that it was a rather unfortunate thing to have said."

Martin laughed again. "I think Fortescue knows me well enough to know I wouldn't disappoint him. Not if he takes me as seriously as all that. He's as good as dead now."

Van Leer laughed, too. "But really, Martin———"

"We'll have to put a notch on that revolver. What did you do with it?"

It came upon Van Leer suddenly that that was perhaps the only way out of it for Martin, to make a joke of it, to laugh it off.

"That's right," he said merrily. "Here it is."

"Regular little old-fashioned six-shooter," said Martin. "Just the thing for partridges. Of .32-caliber—not much noise. What did you do with my nail file?"

"But look here, Martin. There's another thing. You bet Mortimer those ten thousand shares of N. T. C. you'd do it."

"Well, now, don't let that worry you. Can you hear old Mortimer's speech as he presents Fortescue's stuffed head—or was it to be just the horns—to the club? Got that file?"

There was nothing left for Van Leer but to laugh and enter into Martin's mood. "How's that," he said, applying the file. "Is that deep enough? Shall we file a notch for Mortimer, too?"

"No," replied Martin. "We'll just give him plenty of rope and let him hang himself."

They both laughed.

"I guess I'm a little tight, too," said the boy incredulously, and he put the gun back in the pocket of his overcoat.

There was a gleam in Martin's eye as he looked at his watch. It was now exactly seven-thirty o'clock. Everything on schedule to the minute. Not a hitch so far. Two hours and a half more of Van Leer. But dinner at the rate they were being served would take an hour. Then there would be a lot of instructions, directions, details, to talk over. By nine-fifteen they could be starting for the airport. Two stops at saloons were part of the plan. It was all very simple. Van Leer would be out of the way at ten o'clock. He would have disappeared—till he was needed.

But suddenly now Van Leer said, "That reminds me!"

Martin's heart stood still. "What?" he asked coldly.

"Why, the funniest thing! An appointment with Fortescue at eleven-thirty at the club."

"Oh, is that all? Don't worry about that. I'll stop in and see him to-night."

"For goodness' sake, Martin, I wouldn't do that!"

"Why not?" said Martin, smiling. "And here is our dinner at last."

CHAPTER 6

A WOMAN SEES

Something descended upon him, caught in the blast of air.

THE rest was exactly as Field had planned it. At nine-forty-five, he and Freddy were at the airport. Chuck had the plane out on the far end of the field. Van Leer, not quite sober now and almost beyond himself with excitement and boyish spirits, climbed into Martin's flying togs.

"Take care of yourself," said Martin, with true solicitude. "I certainly don't want anything to happen to you."

"Where's my coat?"

"I've got it. You get in."

Martin laid Van Leer's overcoat, with the revolver in the pocket, on the wing of the plane, just out of the boy's reach. Then he went around in front of the plane and took hold of the propeller.

"Switch off."

"Switch off," answered Chuck from the pilot's seat.

Martin turned the engine over.

"Contact."

"Contact."

There was a sputter, followed by a roar. Martin ducked under

34

the wing as the plane wobbled forward. Something descended upon him, caught in the blast of air from the propeller as Chuck, following orders, opened up the throttle. It was the overcoat from the wing. Martin grabbed it. Away roared the plane.

Too easy!

He felt first for the revolver in the pocket of the coat, took it out, made sure of it, feeling the while that it was all a dream. Then he ran back to the car, broke open the box of cartridges, loaded the revolver and deliberately fired a single shot through the floor of the car. Starting the car immediately, he drove furiously across the rough ground of the field toward the main road that would take him back to the city.

He had drunk only what he had planned to drink, but he felt effects strangely more than he had anticipated. His heart was pounding, his head was spinning. But more than anything else his thoughts were racing. They were racing ahead to what he had yet to do and doubling back over the trail of what he had already done.

He had never known his mind so active or so lucid. It was as if danger had sharpened all his perceptions and quickened all his instincts and intuitions. He could see exactly where his chances now stood of getting away with murder. Planned though every step had been, his trail lay marked behind him like footsteps in the snow.

It was, in fact, the planning, the premeditation that involved the act in so much incriminating evidence. Any one might do murder suddenly out-of-hand and escape. That was by far the safest way, though the chances were probably five to one against you. But the planned murder to be watertight must be pretty obvious on the face of it, so many were the contingencies to be provided against.

How could he hope to survive cross-examination on his activities over the past twelve hours? He could see a thousand little points where any story he might make up would be vulnerable. It would be a cinch for Mortimer to involve him in a tangle of lies and contradictions that would end in complete breakdown.

No, nothing like that. There was only one safe way—the one he had planned and must go through with to the end.

This activity of his mind made things about him seem to move slowly. He drove with a false sense of careful deliberation, unaware that he was driving at close to fifty miles an hour. It seemed about twenty. Suddenly he heard a motor-cycle cop pulling up alongside of him, signaling him to stop.

"Arrested for speeding—this does it!" he thought, and knew that it was all over with him now. He had planned for everything but this, this one fatal chance, this something within himself that he could not possibly have foreseen, this acceleration of his thoughts.

But at the same time there was another self that, even while he applied the brakes, was able to search the road ahead for a darker place beneath a tree and between the arc-lights on the brightly lighted boulevard. He stopped there.

"Pretty big hurry, aren't you?" began the cop in the usual manner.

Martin opened the car door and got out. "I'm a doctor on an urgent call, if you don't mind. Here is my license. Doctor Malthus. It's an obstetrical case. And pulling out his wallet he allowed two twenty-dollar bills to drop to the ground.

"You're losing your money," said the cop.

"Never mind. It's life and death. I can't lose any more time than is necessary." He flashed his driver's license. "Is this quite satisfactory? I'll drive a little slower for my own safety."

"But I saw you drop some money—there it blows! Oh, all right, doctor. Only take it easy."

Martin went on his way.

He drove once straight through Fifty-seventh Street directly past his hotel without stopping. Two blocks east of Fifth Avenue he turned around and came back. He parked opposite.

He got out, locked the car and with Van Leer's coat on his arm crossed the street. He made short work of using his latchkey and closing the street door behind him. He took the elevator up to his rooms.

His first act was to hang up Van Leer's overcoat in the coat closet. He smiled to think how hard this would be to have to explain on the witness stand—the coat so neatly hung up. But then it was one of those tracks in the snow that must be obscured by deeper tracks.

He went into the bathroom, drew the shade and turned on the light. Razor and all were ready where he had placed them. He was not a minute removing that dab of mustache. Then he changed his suit, substituting a gray tweed for the blue serge he had been wearing and, having transferred the contents of the pockets, hung the discarded suit over the end of the bed.

All this was on the bare chance that some one had seen him enter the apartment just now and this change of clothes was a small precaution that would tend to discredit such identification.

"I have been here all afternoon—drinking—dead drunk," he told himself.

He went back into the living room, and in the dim light from the street studied the setting. The deep chair, the bottle, the glasses, the littered ash tray, the silver polo cup on the floor, the little jar of caviar—the scene was set. Yes, everything was in place. Perfect!

He took out Fortescue's bunch of keys and selected two, and holding these in his left hand he dipped the thumb and finger tips of his right hand in the caviar. Then with the revolver that Van Leer had bought in his pocket, he descended quickly to Fortescue's door.

It gave him a moment's pause to find a telegram on the floor in front of it. How could that check up? A minor mystery. But his story was to be that he had found the door open when he came in at ten-fifteen. Now what was he going to say? Of course, the messenger boy might not have tried the door, and if the door were not locked—— Even that was improbable.

Martin Field could well see that an affair like this would be shot through with minor mysteries. Perhaps nobody would think about it.

There was something uncanny, too, about that telegram lying there. A message to the dead! What would it say?

He stooped to pick it up, some instinct warning him to read it. But then another instinct, the instinct of a gentleman restrained him. It was one thing to Kill Fortescue, but it was another thing to read his correspondence. He considered destroying the telegram, but in the end he left it lying there...

As he slipped the key in the latch, his nerves played him a horrid trick. He thought he heard the click of a typewriter! A shiver ran down his spine. Would the ghost of Fortescue be sitting there at his desk finishing his love note?

He had to pull himself together.

But if there were some one actually in there——

He tapped softly—waited. Except for the loud pounding of his heart in his ears, there was no sound. He turned the key in the latch, opened the door, stepped quickly across the threshold, and silently closed the door behind him.

The room was hot and a faint feminine perfume hung in the close atmosphere. As nearly as he could see in the dim light from the street, everything was exactly as he remembered having left it.

He'd have to be quick about it now. With eyes not yet accustomed to the darkness, he groped across the room to the flush-paneled door of the bar-closet where he had stowed Fortescue's body. He had the right key this time. The door opened.

The body was there, of course. Martin kicked it with his foot. He caught the glint of staring dead eyes—of teeth in the gaping mouth. Seizing one end of the bearskin rug, he dragged it out to near its original position in the room. Returning to the bar-closet, he examined the floor for evidence of blood. Satisfied, he closed the door and locked it. Then, after carefully wiping the keys clean of fingerprints, put them back in the dead man's waist-coat pocket.

Next he took the revolver from his pocket, wiped it and care-fully imprinted his caviar-greased fingerprints upon it. He laid it on the floor near the body.

How did that look?

One thing more, the crowning satisfaction. The letter! He took it from his pocket and held it up to the light from the street. But he needed no light to read those well remembered lines:

I feel safe in recommending to you the purchase of these ten thousand shares from the Wharton estate, knowing that the Holland International interests are still closely held, that the company is doing very well, and that there are two hundred millions back of the company at any critical juncture.

"You dirty, lying crook!" muttered Martin, and crumpling the letter into a ball, he crammed it into the gaping mouth of the dead man.

As he did so, he experienced a feeling of expiation for all the dumb beasts he had slain.

So strong was this feeling that it held him kneeling there before this enemy he had killed. It held him—or what was it, this sudden creeping paralysis, this icy stillness that bound him rigid. There was something standing over him! Little by little he drew himself back on his heels and looked up.

A beautiful young woman was standing there before him, staring down at him.

CHAPTER 7

NOT ON THE SCHEDULE

Slowly his galvanized muscles relaxed. He caught up the revolver.

IN his astonishment, Martin Field could only kneel there staring back up at the woman, while the silence beat upon him with a rhythmic counting of icy points of time—which presently he knew for the pounding of his heart. He could not move. He was as rigid as the corpse before which he knelt, and over which his hands were still partly outstretched. He could only stare, feeling that all was lost, taking stock of the situation in which he found himself. Caught!

Caught! Yes, nothing left now but a brief experience of being himself a hunted beast, until Mortimer should have run him down. Then the chair.

Slowly his galvanized muscles relaxed. He caught up the revolver.

"If you move or make a sound———" He left his whispered threat unfinished as he thrust the gun against her.

But she made no move. She just stood, her mouth slightly open, looking at him.

Suddenly he felt ridiculous pointing the gun at her. He lowered it. Then with a laugh he stooped and laid it again on the floor beside the body.

"Why, you're just a girl," he said.

She nodded.

"What's that you've got there? Why, that's his gun! Here, give that to me."

Without hesitation, she handed over to him the little nickel-plated Smith & Wesson. And as she came nearer, his eyes, accustomed to the darkness, took in the slender yet beautifully rounded figure with the narrow shoulders and small, delicate white hand held out toward him.

"What are you doing here? How did you get in?"

The lovely face that had been lifted to his was quickly turned away. The outstretched hand from which he had taken the revolver fell to her side. That was answer enough.

"Latchkey?"

She nodded her hung head. He noted a prudency as always unnecessary. Women were brazen at heart.

Field laughed at her.

Instantly then she changed, stiffened, and said in a whisper, "I came here to kill him! I've been waiting for hours here in the dark to kill him when he came in."

"Well I'll be damned!" ejaculated Martin.

Now they stood for a long moment facing each other, saying nothing. A desire to laugh possessed Martin. But this passed as he grew aware of the fixity of her gaze upon him. He finally said, and it sounded rather silly:

"What are you looking at me like that for?"—as if he, too, should have hung his head. "I suppose this is rather awful. But he was out gunning for me, too."

Again there fell a silence, like an awkward pause in a dinner conversation that would have been broken by a reference to the weather.

"Well, you don't have to stare at me so," he protested absurdly. "You're eyewitness enough. My God!"

A realization of his ghastly failure beat in upon him at his own words. "Eyewitness," he repeated incredulous of such a slip-up. "Eyewitness— my God!"

"No, no! *I* meant to do it. *I* meant——"

He laughed.

"No, it's the truth!"

"Well, I'm taking no chances on it. Suppose we cut the formalities. I'm in a desperate hurry! You think you've got me where

I'll have to pay. That, at least, makes sense. But don't fool yourself I've got my alibi, and all I'm going to do now is to call the police and pin it on you."

It was as if she had expected it. She shivered as she said simply, "O. K."

"What do you mean by that?"

"You'll be safe enough saying I did it. I haven't any alibi. I've been walking the streets for hours."

He paused to digest that.

"You're just wasting time—stalling."

"No."

"Well, it's your life or mine. I'm very sorry. Your latchkey let you in for something this time."

"That's all right." Her voice quivered, but she stood curiously resolute. "Only please don't call the police for—for just a moment."

"You must be crazy."

"Oh, don't scold me!"

"For Pete's sake——"

"I'm awfully frightened."

She was swaying. He reached without ceremony and caught her in his hands.

"Here, cut this. I haven't any time for it!"

She wilted a little in that grip. He relaxed his hold quickly. She felt soft to his touch and he noted how her hands clung womanlike to his arm.

Blackmail was the one thought evoked by that contact. He could never think of a woman in any other way—not since that ridiculous breach-of-promise suit of fifteen years ago.

"All right," he said. "How much do you want?"

She stiffened as if he had struck her.

"How much? How much?" he repeated.

She gasped. "Just time—time to get my courage."

"If you're stalling till somebody gets • here, you're crazy. You're the one that's in on this—with your little latchkey. Of course, I'd hate to do it, but—— Let's not talk about that. How much do you want? That's your best game. I'll pay. Only you've got to be quick." He was shaking her. "Come on. How much? Twenty-five thousand dollars?"

No reply.

Desperately he thought of saying fifty thousand—even a hundred. It was the price of his life. There was no time at all What could he do? He felt suddenly completely lost. His demoniac presence of mind had failed him at last.

Not in a thousand years could he have reasoned out why he did what he did. Something altogether alien to all his convictions impelled him. He drew her suddenly close in his arms and bent his face to hers.

"Here now," he whispered. "You get out of here. This is my affair."

She sighed and seemed to melt toward him into his closer embrace. And he permitted a minute or two to pass before he spoke.

"On your way."

For there was suddenly no question left in his mind about believing her. He quite simply believed her.

But again he felt her draw back from him, her whole slender body becoming taut; felt the expansion of her lovely breast as she took a long breath, tremulously, and seemed to hold it indefinitely. Was she going to scream? He raised his hand to cover her mouth, but then she spoke.

"You go! You!"

It surprised him into a laugh.

"But I meant to kill him!" she cried. "I was waiting to kill him. It was right for me to do it. It was the only thing left me. Don't you see——?"

He cut her short.

"That's all very well, but you didn't kill him. I did, and you've got to get out."

"Thanks. But I'm not going to. It's easier than going over it again and again. I can't stand it. I know what I'm doing. Killing yourself is no cinch. But this is simple. Now you can call the police as you said you would."

Martin's despair grew a shade blacker.

"Damn you, you fool little girl!" he flung at her savagely. "You'll do exactly what I tell you."

His ferocity did it. Her resistance broke. The whole look of her changed.

"But I've no place to go," she said in a numb tone.

Had God created anything so inconsequential as woman!

"Oh, yes, you have. And it's out of here. You're not going to be mixed up in this."

"But I am—hopelessly. It's all a hopeless mess for me. Don't you understand? What's the matter with you, anyway?"

It was as if he had only aroused her courage anew to obstruct him. Somehow, she now seemed to have the better of him. He ran his fingers through his hair.

"So that's it."

"That's it. As they used to say in old-fashioned novels, I've been 'betrayed.' "

"You poor kid."

"It's the easiest way out of it for me. I've had three months of hell. I hadn't the courage to jump off the bridge. Sounds silly, but I'm afraid of heights. And I'm afraid of guns, too."

A thought stirred in Martin's mind, troubling his conscience for the first time. "I killed the man who might have made things right for you," he said solemnly.

"Oh, he wasn't that kind."

"I suppose not. But God knows you're very lovely. And you're young. And I'd say you were a 'good' girl till you got mixed up with him. He could have done a lot worse."

His tone on the last three words was slightly contemptuous.

"You hate women, don't you?"

"What has that to do with it?"

She laughed.

But he had no time to find her meaning. The minutes were precious.

"It's up to me to assume his obligations," he said bluntly. "Let's not argue about it. That's that. And this having no place to go and nothing to live for—I'm going to see to all that. What's money? I'll give you enough to go straight from here to Timbuctoo if you'll only get going."

She shook her head, smiled, bent her face to his shoulder. He felt moved again, but reacted instantly, raising his old defenses against sentiment.

"That way out isn't any way out for me," she said. "There's no way out that leads to—well, to Timbuctoo. I'd call that just getting deeper and deeper. I'd thought of it, of course. I'm two months ahead of you thinking about it. I know what I'm doing."

Martin groaned. He felt like a man in a fog who could make no headway. But suddenly there came to him a glimmer of sense.

"Are you trying to save me? Is that what you're up to?"

She raised her face. "Well, it's got to be one of us—you or me. You said that yourself."

He drew a deep breath of relief.

"So that's it! Well, get this. You're not doing a thing for me but sending me to the chair. I've got this whole thing framed —except for you being here. I just want you to get out and keep out."

"No! No! You don't know. They'd be sure to get you. You

haven't a chance."

"Not with you under my feet."

He had spoken brutally under the stress of desperation. But immediately the gentleman in him retracted.

"I'm sorry. But don't you see I can't accept your proposition —sensible as it may seem to you. There's no way out for me that isn't also your way out. If it's just a name for a child—his child —I'll make that up to you. And I'll say this for you, you poor little kid, you've got something that gets me. All right. And don't think I'm not grateful or that there's anything I've got to give that I won't give you. Sounds absurd, of course, after what you are offering me. But, then, that's all nonsense. You don't want to die. And I don't want you to die. You're a sweet kid. Things like this are easily fixed."

She had drawn back from him and the darkness was between them. But now he heard her crying.

At sound of it a new terror seized him. Hysteria! He stepped forward and caught her roughly in his arms. "Cut it out! I tell you to cut it out! Get hold of yourself!"

Again he felt the jerking of her ribs, the sobs that meant for him the collapse of her heroism. Her nerves had carried her as far as they would.

"Listen," he commanded, "you're now going to do exactly what I tell you. Do you understand that?"

He shook her, and as he shook her she stopped crying: she went limp in his hands so that he had to hold her up. Then she clung to him.

"Oh, I'm so frightened!" she whispered at last.

He knew that he was safe then. It was only a matter of smoothing her down. But what a break! His schedule was all shot to pieces.

"There! There! Get hold of yourself or we're both lost."

Strength seemed to come again to her small body.

"All right."

"That's the girl! We must clear your tracks out of here. You'll want some money. Here—never mind counting it! Take a bus to Boston and stay there for a while. Don't be afraid. After it's all over let me know where you are. What's your name?"

"Gretchen Demarest."

"Mine's Martin Field. Now don't forget it."

She followed him to the door. He opened it, listened and peered into the hall.

"All clear! Get out quickly. But don't run. You'll be seen, perhaps. Never mind. Go straight to the nearest drug store and call the police. Don't give your name. Only be quick about it. My life depends on you."

She made no answer. But she gently pushed the door wider open so that the light from the hall fell upon them. For a few seconds they stood looking for the first time into each other's eyes. Then she smiled and, reaching up, kissed him very simply on the cheek. She was gone.

He heard the elevator wheezing downward as he released the latch on the door and, leaving it wide open, scurried back up to his own rooms. His own door he left ajar, and, flinging himself into the chair by the table with the bottles and glasses, proceeded to pour and swallow one drink after another until the room swam dizzily about him. Still he poured liquor into himself, drink after drink.

Would it ever take hold? He drank water. Then more whisky. He emptied the bottle. It fell from his hand and rolled on the floor. He took up another bottle—spilled half a glassful over himself, but continued drinking as fast as he could put the stuff down him.

It was not so easy. It choked him, burned his throat. He began to feel sick. But would he ever become drunk—dead drunk and insensible? *Fffff*—the taste of whisky! Gin was easier. He groped for the square bottle.

Then he heard the police sirens. Here they were now, the police. They'd be up for him before the damned stuff took effect. "Perfly shober," he said and put the gin bottle to his lips. He took one swallow and——

CHAPTER 8

ACCUSED!

"Where am I?" Martin asked. "You're in jail," replied the narrow white woman.

MARTIN came to by stages. He was conscious first of a complete and overwhelming misery. He groaned and struck blindly about him at all sorts of crawling things. Then a vast weight fell upon him and bore him down, down, down into a cavernous place where, in a sizzling calm, people were floating around him.

His head ached. He could not move his arms. They were in a strait-jacket. He heard voices, but could not focus his mind on what they were saying. He tried to speak, but immediately everything went far off and became small and old, tired, worn, and heavy. And the doctor said, "That'll quiet him. Let him sleep. He'll pull round."

When Martin next awoke he found himself in a narrow white cot in a narrow white room being watched by a narrow white woman sitting stiffly in a narrow white chair.

"Where am I?" he asked.

"You're in jail." She was nothing if not to the point.

She got up at once and went into the hall.

Two policemen replaced her.

"Where am I?"

"Jail."

"Jail? What for?"

The one policeman who did the talking was also curt and to the point. "Murder."

"Murder? You mean I killed some one?"

"I'll say you did."

"Must have been an accident. I don't remember a thing."

"Remember getting drunk, don't you?"

Martin could remember nothing. He tried his best. "Drunk? Why, yes. I was on a boat—at the races. No, that was—— When was that? I mean when is this? I don't seem to be able to connect up."

"Remember your name, don't you?"

"Of course."

"Remember where you were last Saturday, don't you?"

"What Saturday was that?"

Nothing at all connected up in Martin's brain. His mind was perfectly clear, but it floated airily in time and space.

The policeman thrust his red face into Martin's.

"*Last Saturday.* Come on, now. *Last Saturday.*"

Bits of a hundred Saturdays spattered the focus of Martin's memory and were drawn there into a pattern of the typical Saturday, a thing of half days on the exchange and escapes from the city to the country, the restrained beginnings of binges, tangled bits of back-stage life, distorted fragments of night clubs, football games, boat races. Saturday was an institution of civilized life. It had no existence in the bush, or on the high seas. In the woods there were no days of the week. In the woods! "Now I remember," he said. "I was up shooting at my place in Canada."

"You mean you'd just got back. Well, go on from there."

"That's right. I came back—flew back. There was something about somebody mixed up with a white black bear. Yes, and getting a gun and an awfully pretty girl named Gretchen. And sending some one off to camp. And a wonderful plan with caviar and fingerprints——"

The policeman rose and went out into the hall and spoke to what might have been a large number of persons.

"He'll talk. Get District Attorney Mortimer." A pause. "Well, find him and be quick about it."

Mortimer!

The fragments began to whirl and jiggle and come together in order like a cinema caption. Memory suddenly came back to Martin. He had killed Fortescue. He remembered it now in perfect detail.

But what had he said to the policeman? He sat up in his narrow white cot in panic. Plan—cavier—fingerprints!

Good heavens, how close he had come to giving himself away!

It was not many minutes before District Attorney Mortimer got there.

"Well, here we are," he began in his most crushing tone. And it seemed to Martin that all Mortimer needed was a pith helmet and a rifle and his foot on his, Martin's, prostrate body to complete the pose.

"Perhaps you don't know where you are yet. You're in jail, charged with the murder of Creighton Fortescue. You must have been crazy drunk, to say that much for you. I don't suppose you remember much about it."

"Not a thing. But I don't believe you. Don't be an ass, Mortimer. How did I——"

"Oh, it's all as plain as print. You should never touch strong drink, my boy. You don't know what you are doing. But the law takes no cognizance of that. It's the chair for you. Might as well know the worst."

And as Martin continued dumb, Mortimer went on to describe with great accuracy what the police had found. First the obvious things: Fortescue dead—dead for about six hours, the coroner and the doctor had said. And then the revolver with the caviar fingerprints on it.

"Your fingerprints, Field. And your revolver, I suppose. Not much use denying it. Colt .32 Police Positive."

"Good heavens!" said Martin.

"But that isn't all." Mortimer was enjoying this. "There was that letter, the letter you boasted you'd choke him with, crammed in his mouth! You don't remember doing that? Too bad! It must have been such a satisfaction—at the time. Rather to be regretted from your present situation."

Martin held his head in his hands. "I don't remember a thing."

"Well, there you are. The police found you up in your rooms. And were you a mess? Oh, boy! You must have set out to break the world's championship Marathon solitary drinking record. We got a picture of you. Hi, Mike, let's have that *Mirror* with the picture of Field drunk! Here you are. Take a look at yourself."

Martin glanced at the newspaper and then covered his face with his hands.

"The easiest way out of this is for you to sign a confession. It's an open-and-shut case for the State. The proof is all right there. How about it?"

Martin changed his tone. "Very well then, if I did kill him, that's that. I don't remember a thing, and I don't want to remember."

"You know, of course, that that won't get you anywhere in court."

"I know. But it's a lot more decent. Go ahead and get the trial over. I won't put in any defense. I won't fight. Just mark it 'Rush,' will you?"

"Oh, it'll be quick enough," said Mortimer. "Don't worry about that. But a signed confession is the simplest way to go at it."

"Damn you, Mortimer, I've told you that I don't remember a thing. That's my only defense—a defense of my self-respect. You can leave me that. I don't seem to be able to remember what day it is, or where I left off remembering."

"It will come back to you," said Mortimer, smiling. "You remember getting drunk, don't you?"

"Of course—but when?"

"Last Saturday."

Martin rubbed his forehead. "Saturday? I sometimes play squash on Saturdays. Or else poker. I sort of remember sitting in on a game that went on all night."

"Not that Saturday, old man. Nothing like that. I'll have to start you off. Let me see. You'd been away. Yes, you wisely pulled your freight right after you'd shot your face off at the club that afternoon, saying you'd add Fortescue to your collection of stuffed heads. I suppose you went up to your Canada place where the reporters couldn't get at you. Well, you flew down Friday night and got here Saturday morning. Probably had a flask with you. Or were you too drunk to remember even that?"

Martin shook his head.

"It'll all come back to you in time," continued Mortimer remorselessly. "Well, then, you turned up in town on Saturday morning and went straight to your room. And there you stayed afraid to show your face to get up your courage to put in an appearance at the club. But you didn't have the nerve—after the fool you'd made of yourself.

"So you had a couple more to blot that out and then you got out Fortescue's letter and got yourself nicely worked up. You were probably completely pie-eyed by that time. That was a little after half past five. They heard the shot in the room below. It was in the middle of the Peristalto hour on the radio. In fact, that times the killing of Creighton Fortescue to the minute."

"Go on."

"But there's the whole story. Some one of Fortescue's girl friends called the police. That was about ten-thirty. And were you drunk when we found you? Here it is Tuesday. We've been over two days thawing you out."

"It's all some damn trick of yours!" cried Martin. "You think you can pin this thing on me. Well, you can't!"

"I thought you'd show some fight," replied Mortimer.

"I dare say you'd like a chance to show off," flared Martin. "A chance to pull a lot of bits like that about the radio."

Mortimer smiled. "Elementary, my dear *Watson*. Elementary."

"So that's your idea, isn't it—to score off me? Well, to hell with you, you swine! I meant to kill Fortescue, and I'm glad I did kill him. It's too bad I don't remember doing it. But I don't, and that's all the defense you'll ever get out of me."

Mortimer clicked his tongue.

"Who's going to defend you, old man? Not that it matters. But he'll be able to attend to your will and all the grim details like the undertaker. I believe embalming is quite difficult after electrocution. Better be cremated; it carries the process to a logical completion. And while you're fixing up your will, don't forget that little matter of the ten thousand shares of N. T. C."

"Thanks for reminding me," said Martin. "But I hadn't forgotten that bet. What was it you were going to do? Frame the letter and present it to the club with a proper speech—that is, of course, only if I could get away with it. Swell idea, wasn't it?"

"I don't think you've quite come to yet," said Mortimer.

"Oh, yes, I have. And I'll bet you another ten thousand shares, you common hangman, ten thousand shares against ten buttons off your pants that you won't pull the switch yourself."

Mortimer flinched at this, but after a moment's reflection he said, "I'll take that one, too." And turning to the policeman behind him gave his order:

"Get him out of here."

CHAPTER 9

STUBBORN CLIENT

"What in hell's holding up my trial?" shouted Martin.

MURDERER! Martin had reflected upon it in his cell. It was not a pleasant word to have applied to you in a society shot through with hypocrisy and sentimentality. But Martin was above all that. He saw Manhattan as but another sort of jungle in which one fought — not with poisoned darts, but with due processes of law. He had lived too long among savages in the jungle to feel the taboo of murder. He had killed Fortescue as he would have killed a wild beast. Far from feeling any remorse for the act, he felt rather an exaltation, a sense of expiation.

But he knew that so-called honest people would shun him now if they knew that he had committed murder, even though he had rid this society of theirs of a lecherous swindler like Fortescue. And they would honor a cold-blooded hangman like Mortimer who upheld their law. A natural savage!

He paused and then retracted this. No, not a savage. Martin had lived a large part of his life among savages and he respected them. Yes, he respected the judgment of a man's just anger above any and all laws made by man.

Stigma! These newspapers with their screaming headlines and

photographs! How awful they were!

Here was a test of character. A man of any force of character ought to rise on his own honest convictions above all that.

The newspapers, he was glad to see, left very little for the State to do. Martin found himself tried and convicted out of hand. This was exactly what he wanted.

The first half dozen lawyers he asked to defend him made their excuses. Excellent! His case was regarded as hopeless. He sent word of this to Mortimer, asking for an immediate trial, for the State to appoint counsel to defend him—and at the same time refusing to enter any defense.

This, too, went to the papers, and he was pleased to see the spirit in which it was taken. They regarded it as an act of extraordinary fortitude, coupled with an honest man's decent respect for their law, and decent shame for his own foul deed.

It was all beginning to be highly amusing.

At the indictment, Martin fairly confounded the press by his willingness to be photographed. Handsome, that lean brown face of his with his white teeth so very white as he smiled! And he was always smiling. Nobody saw anything enigmatic in that smile, least of all District Attorney Mortimer. If the smile signified anything, it was pure bravado. And bravado always takes.

Martin clicked his tongue over the rush of would-be widows that followed the syndication of these pictures. He sent a bundle of these letters to Mortimer with a note. "What about the motion-picture rights of the electrocution?"

"That fellow has his nerve," said Mortimer. But nothing that Martin did put him on his guard.

The lawyer appointed by the court to defend Martin was perfunctory. Martin persisted in remembering nothing. When pressed by this Mr. Burgundy, he would recall disconnected bits of many Saturdays. He could remember only that he had been up in the woods and that he had flown back. He remembered getting out of the plane at the flying field. But was it last Saturday? He had done all this so many times.

Under pressure, he would follow some train of events to a football game at Princeton, or out to Short Hills for a week-end. He could remember going to his apartment, of course, and he could remember taking a few drinks—but which time was that?

"Hopeless!" declared the exasperated Mr. Burgundy. "You might just as well plead guilty."

"How can I plead guilty unless I remember?" insisted Martin. I don't remember a damn thing. And, to tell the truth, I don't especially want to remember anything. Why should I? As it is, I have no conscious responsibility for my act. Let it stand at that."

"That's all very pretty, but it won't get you off the death penalty."

"Oh, no, of course not. But it mitigates the stigma," argued Martin. "This trial is just my final gesture. Well, then, I'm for making it a fine flourish. Lots of bravado, that's the idea. Why, the papers are eating it up. And popular sympathy is all in my favor—immoral as it may seem."

"But it won't keep you from going to the chair," expostulated Mr. Burgundy.

"Why bring that up? What I want is quick action. Mortimer will keep me here as long as he can, just to gloat. What's the chair to being locked up here? Well, this growing popular sympathy is the one thing that will force Mortimer's hand. He won't like it."

Mr. Burgundy muttered an imprecation. "This sort of case they have to hand me!"

"I admit that I'm not thinking of you," said Martin acidly.

"There's my reputation——"

"If you think that it will do your reputation any good to try and put up a defense instead of a *nolo contendere*——"

"So. I might do worse."

"Never mind the defense. All I want is my constitutional rights to immediate trial. If I'm paying you for anything, it's for that," said Martin, pacing his cell.

Mr. Burgundy shrugged shoulders. "You're paying me."

Martin had discounted the law's delay. Delay was the one serious chance that he must take. He could feel confident of keeping Van Leer out of the way for three weeks. After that it was up to Chuck.

He could only place a reasonable dependence on Chuck. He had given the boy orders to make Van Leer comfortable and to provide him with sport. If Van Leer got restless, it was up to Chuck to discover some excuse for keeping him. Van Leer was to remain a guest, or a prisoner, till Martin sent word to Chuck. And it was no business of Chuck's to ask why.

Martin wanted no accomplices. Orders were orders. Hold Van Leer. Take good care of him. No radio. No newspapers. No visitors. Avoid strangers. Keep in the woods. Under no circumstances was Chuck to leave Freddy. No, it was quite as important to keep Chuck out of touch with the world as it was to impound Van Leer. Martin wondered how Chuck would react to the news that his boss was in jail for murder. Would orders hold, or would

the boy come winging back with· Van Leer—*too soon?*

Martin paced his cell night after night.

Mortimer was suspicious. "Immediate trial. Constitutional rights. *Nolo contendere.* What's his game?" he asked, looking across his desk at Mr. Burgundy.

"That you should know," snorted the lawyer for the defense.

"I had nothing to do with your appointment to this case," replied Mortimer. "And if I had, you should have been glad to get it. There's no work and there's fair publicity. And a fat fee."

Mr. Burgundy spread his hands in a gesture of resignation.

"One of these days, Mortimer, I'll show you."   •

"Stow it, Felix. How did I know he'd lie down on you like this? Of course, it spoils my sport, too. I was counting on having some fun with him on the witness stand."

"As drunk as he was—you expect him to remember anything?" ejaculated Burgundy with sarcasm. "You're smart. Well, I'll tell you another thing: he knows better than to try to remember anything. If you're waiting for that to happen to——"

"No, no. I quite realize his position. But I'd like to jolt some memory into him. Immediate trial and constitutional rights be damned! I'll hold him till he does remember. I'll make him show fight one way or another."

"So?" returned Burgundy. "You'll hold him till the governor pardons him in order to keep the women's vote."

Mortimer scowled. "Yes, there's that. But who cares what the papers say? He stands convicted already. There's nothing to it, Burgundy. Nothing. He'll get the chair no matter what the popular sympathy is. Damn it, there isn't any case. Why don't you do something? *Nolo contendere!* Can't you even put up your hands? Why don't you cook up an alibi? You could prove he was having tea with his aunt or—— Say, what happened to that pilot of his? There's a line for you."

"Yah!" snorted Burgundy. "So you could tell me something?"

Mortimer laughed. "I didn't mean it that way, Burgundy. As a matter of fact, I can tell you as much as the police have found out, if it would be of any help to you. We haven't followed the thing up, merely because the State's case is complete without any further evidence. The fellow's name is Chuck Vaisseau. He's a French Canadian. He flew in at the Jersey City airport at about six a. m. on Saturday. Hung around there all day, and took off at nine or ten o'clock that night."

"Thanks," said Burgundy. "I suppose you'd like me to tell you now what I know. Well, since it interests you, Martin Field remembers paying Chuck off. The boy goes back to trapping in the winter. Comes from the Providence of Quebec. Might take some little time to find him. But what's to prevent the defense from putting it up to the State to produce him as a witness?"

This proposition took Mortimer a little by surprise. "Of course," he began, "it might take all winter to find him. I thought Martin Field wanted an immediate trial. Perhaps my suggestion——"

"You can take your suggestions and go jump in the lake," snorted Mr. Burgundy. "It's a lousy case for me, and you know it. Do you think I'm going to make a monkey of myself so that you can show off? No, sir! I'm ready to go to court tomorrow. I demand for my client an immediate trial."

"O. K.," said the district attorney. "You'll get it."

But even so it was three weeks before the case was called.

Martin fumed and walked his cell. A man of excess physical energy, accustomed to life in the open, the constriction of his cell drove him nearly mad. Every day he was taken from the cell to the little room where he conferred with his lawyer. And every day he found it a little harder to maintain that outward stoicism upon which his life depended.

Mr. Burgundy continued to fuss about his reputation. He seemed to think that as counsel for the defense he ought to be able to do something. He might enter a plea of insanity, but Martin would not hear of it. Any other defense was quite hopeless. The daily conference was generally brief.

"You still don't remember anything?"

Martin would merely shake his head.

And while Martin shook, Mr. Burgundy nodded.

"Yah! Under the circumstances—— Well, any day now."

Once Martin's nerves got the better of him. "Any day! What in hell's keeping him? Hasn't he got enough evidence? I ask for an immediate trial, and I'm kept cooped up for weeks! Don't you understand, it's got to be quick. Everything depends on—on——"

"On what?" queried his lawyer.

"On not remembering."

Mr. Burgundy agreed with him on that point.

On the third Saturday following Fortescue's death, Mr. Burgundy brought word to Martin's cell that the case was called for the coming Monday.

CHAPTER 10

CODE MESSAGE

Mortimer opened up with great vigor upon the first talesman.

AND so on the twenty-third day following the murder of Creighton Fortescue, Martin Field was brought to trial. Handcuffed, he was taken from his cell to the crowded courtroom; the handcuffs were removed and he found himself seated between Mr. Burgundy and his very slick young assistant.

The clerk immediately called the court to order, the charges were read, Mr. Burgundy responded with a plea of not guilty, and action began with the selection of a jury.

Mortimer, very dapper with a gardenia in his buttonhole, opened up with great vigor upon the first talesman, a watery-eyed bookkeeper suffering from a bad cold in the head. After prolonged and rather unnecessary cross-questioning upon this poor fellow's convictions regarding capital punishment, Mortimer accepted him and yielded the floor to the defense.

Mr. Burgundy hardly rose from his seat.

"The defense accepts this juror."

So it went with all twelve good men and true—four of whom happened to be women.

The whole jury was selected in less than an hour.

The judge at this point intervened. Turning first to Mr. Burgundy, he inquired whether the defense, having pleaded not guilty, were or were not going to contest the charges.

Mr. Burgundy rose and replied in that courtroom rhetoric so different from his daily speech.

"The defense will contest the charges; the contention being, in brief, that the defendant has no remembrance whatsoever of the acts of which he is charged and for which he is held and to which charges he must now answer in this court before this jury for his life."

"That, I take it, will be brief," said the judge. "And now may I ask the district attorney how much time the prosecution will require to put its case—that is, at an estimate?"

"I shall probably require a day for the examination of witnesses and the presentation of evidence, and a few hours to sum up—certainly not more," Mortimer replied.

The judge nodded. "Thank you, gentlemen. This case has been interpolated upon a crowded session. That it would be of short duration was a reasonable presumption. The officer of the court is instructed to provide for the jury, see that they are properly lodged and kept incommunicado, to which purpose court is herewith adjourned till ten o'clock to-morrow."

At the stroke of the gavel Martin was on his feet.

"Two days! Hell's bells, I'd counted on his putting on a bigger show than that," he whispered to the astonished Mr. Burgundy.

"What kind of a show do you think this is?"

"But he's cutting me pretty short! I must have a talk with you right away."

Back in his cell, Martin did some quick thinking. Two days—only forty-eight hours before the case would go to the jury. His plan required a minimum of twelve hours, but it was safer to allow fifteen hours. Seventeen hours on the outside. The first four hours would have to be daylight. Twelve o'clock now—that would leave him yet an hour and a half, possibly two hours before he would have to put off doing anything till the next day. He must make up his mind at once.

Flying conditions were a prime factor. He turned the pages of the morning paper to the meteorological column where he read that weather conditions for northern New York were perfect. Clear and slightly colder. Early November weather.

No hitch there. What was to be done would be done with perfect expedition; he had seen to that. If you put enough money back of a thing—— Seventeen hours at the outside. That would bring it to five o'clock to-morrow morning. That would be too soon. But, no. A subpoena would fix that. Might be a little hard to explain. It would be better to wait till to-morrow. Take a chance? Well, no, not exactly a chance, because he could always stall. A slight return of memory. But that would spoil the effect.

The effect! Mortimer with his damned gardenia, and all that wonderful evidence! Suddenly Martin began to laugh. Priceless!

He was barely able to control himself before Mr. Burgundy got to him. They adjourned at once to the tomb-like chamber where they held their daily conferences.

"Do you suppose there is any likelihood of anybody eavesdropping, Burgundy?"

"Not likely," said the lawyer.

"Do you suppose I could make a telephone call?" He pointed to a telephone on a table in the corner of the room.

"It will all be reported to Mortimer, of course."

Martin smiled. "I suppose so. And I suppose that if I called my secretary and said *Eenie, meenie, minee, mo* to her Mortimer would subpoena her immediately."

"Probably, or rather undoubtedly. What would that message mean?"

"Nothing at all. I was just curious. It is really quite a swell idea, Burgundy. I wonder how far Mortimer would go? Suppose we should call everybody I know in town, what a turn-out we'd have—provided Mortimer subpoenaed them all. He'd have to stop somewhere, wouldn't he? I don't suppose there's a Social Register in this jail? Well, not to miss any one let's start on 'A.' Who'll be our *Abu Ben Adhem* to lead all the rest? Alexander Albro.

"Here goes!

"Hello! Switchboard! Hello, who is this? Sergeant Cook. . . . Martin Field speaking. I want to call a few outside numbers. I say. . . . Hello! Now who is this? Captain Tailer. . . . Martin Field speaking. I want to call. . . . Hello, hello! . . . Oh, warden, Martin Field speaking. Yes, charged with killing Creighton Fortescue— murder most foul. In the matter of my defense I want to call some outside numbers without any one listening in. . . . Oh, I see. Naturally not, warden. I suppose every place has its traditions. Rules are rules, aren't they? . . . Yes, yes; I'll speak to my lawyer. Thank you."

"Say," sputtered Mr. Burgundy, "where do you think you are?"

"Just a precaution, Burgundy," said Martin scribbling names on a sheet of paper. "We want to make this party *recherche*, don't we?" He struck out a name he had just written. "You'll have to get everybody in your office busy on this, Burgundy: If Mortimer is as smart as you think he is, he'll have them all subpoenaed. And what a party that will be!"

"I begin to see what you are driving at," said Mr. Burgundy. "But I can assure you any message you wish to transmit through my office will not fall into Mortimer's hands."

"No telephone call is safe—especially long distance. If for example, I should ask you to call Mr. John Smith of Chicago and say briefly, 'Get going,' how long do you suppose it would be before Mortimer would have the matter in the hands of the Chicago police?"

"I don't for a minute believe he would know a thing about it. You'd be perfectly safe."

Martin smiled. "Shall we make an experiment? And by the way, it is hardly probable that the police would have a microphone in this room."

"Impossible," replied the lawyer. "Anything like that would be grounds for a mistrial."

"Well, then, it will be a fair experiment. You will call from your office—no, from your own home. He wrote a name and a Montreal telephone number. "Don't mention any names. Just say it is for Account 3 X. Buy fifty thousand shares H. I. P. at the market.

Make it short and suspicious. No names. And remember to ask about the weather. That'll confuse Mortimer."

Two hours later a note was brought to Martin's cell. It was brief.

"*Weather just right.*"

Martin reiterated his "Too easy." His code message had got through.

There was only the barest possibility that any investigation of this call would reveal its real nature. It was worth five hundred dollars to a young aviator in Montreal to make a familiar three-hour flight and to deliver a simple code message.

While nothing in life was certain, there was every probability that Frederick van Leer would be back in New York City before one o'clock the following afternoon.

CHAPTER 11

"THE PROSECUTION RESTS!"

Townsend as first witness would start the trial off with just the right tone.

MORTIMER opened the case for the State with a brief, bold anticlimatic summary. There was, he said, no disputing the fact that Martin Field had killed Creighton Fortescue. The defendant had been caught practically *in delitu*—red-handed. It was quite inconceivable that the defense would offer any denial.

He went on in a more virulent strain. This was murder inspired by vengeance. It was soberly premeditated and perpetrated under the cowardly stimulation of liquor. He recalled the episode at the club five weeks previously, when Martin Field had bragged before witnesses that he would kill Creighton Fortescue by choking him with a certain letter.

On the night of October 17th at 10:45 p. m. the police, summoned by a mysterious woman's voice, had found the dead body of Creighton Fortescue in his apartment with this same letter crammed into his mouth. There was also a revolver beside the body and upon the revolver were fingerprints positively identified as those of the defendant. They had also found Martin Field insensible with liquor in his rooms two floors above those of

Creighton Fortescue.

There was incontestable proof, furthermore, that Martin Field had returned to the city that same day, that he had returned for no other purpose than to kill Creighton Fortescue, that he had lain in wait for him. It was all a matter of incontestable evidence. The State would, therefore, begin without more ado by calling its first witness, Mr. Peter Townsend.

Martin smiled. Townsend in the witness chair would start the trial off with just the right tone. Tall, slender, aristocratic; white mustache, erect military bearing; raising a gloved hand to take the oath in that slightly Oxford accent—perfect, thought Martin. This was going to be a beautiful trial. He noticed Mortimer adjusting his gardenia as he began the examination.

A few direct questions settled matters of place, date, time of day, after which Townsend was permitted to tell in his own words exactly what had happened at the club on that fatal afternoon.

"Thank you," said Mortimer, and, turning to Mr. Burgundy, "Your witness."

Martin whispered to Burgundy; then the lawyer for the defense rose.

"I should like to ask the witness to repeat the term of opprobrium, as he calls it, that, so he testifies, was applied by the defendant to the district attorney."

"Dumb ass."

" 'Dumb ass'?"

"I said, 'Dumb ass,' " repeated Townsend.

"That will satisfy the defense," said Mr. Burgundy.

The first titter of laughter ran through the courtroom.

The State now called two other members of the club to the witness chair. These two briefly corroborated Townsend's testimony. To each one the defense put the same question pertaining to the "term of opprobrium," and at each repetition of the epithet the laughter grew.

The judge rapped for order.

Mortimer, visibly nettled, called no more club members to the stand. His next witness was an attendant from the flying field whose brief testimony substantiated the fact of Martin's arrival by plane at Jersey City on the morning of the murder.

Mortimer then called the occupants of the suite directly below Fortescue's. These proved to be a theatrical impresario, an elf of a man, and his ex-grand-opera wife of generous proportions. Each in turn on the stand testified to having heard the shot, which they had mistaken for a slammed door. It had caused them to miss the point of what one comedian had said to the other comedian. Mortimer read from some pages of yellow script:

"Doan yo' know, boy, dat ef yo' a genelman yo' gits up when a lady come in de room? Doan yo' know dat?"

"Sho Ah know dat. But what Ah cain't figger out is how Ah kin stand up when Ah got another lady settin' on my lap What Ah do den?"

"De book don' say dat. De book say dat a genelman bound to reespect any lady. Yo' know how it's de woman dat pays and pays."

"Yassah, Ah know dat. Ony mah wife she don' pay cash. She charges it."

The ex-grand-opera contralto, still on the stand, interrupted.

"Right there, Mr. District Attorney. Where he said 'She charges it.'"

"Which exactly times the spot that killed Creighton Fortescue. It was fired at five thirty-three p. m.," said Mortimer, twiddling his gardenia.

The judge now rose and the clerk called the noon recess.

Handcuffed again, Martin was taken out of the courtroom. In the corridor a group of reporters waylaid him. Martin posed smiling while a dozen flash lamps flashed.

Alone for a moment with Burgundy, he said suddenly:

"Funny, but as I recall that episode at the club there was another member, a young fellow named—let me think—Van Leer. He was with Townsend. Why do you supposed Mortimer didn't put him on the stand?"

The lawyer spread his hands. "He had all the witnesses he needed. What does it matter to you?"

"Nothing, of course. But for some reason I seem to remember Van Leer as having some part in all this, I can't think what. But there's some association. That's why I question Mortimer's not having called him. Possibly the boy is out of town. He was waiting for a consular appointment. But there is something else I can't seem to remember. Something right in the back of my head, Burgundy. I'd just like you to find out if he is in town. Twelve o'clock, isn't it? Try the club."

"What did you say his name was?"

"Fred van Leer."

Mr. Burgundy made a note on the back of an envelope.

When court reconvened, Burgundy whispered in Martin's ear. "You're right. That Van Leer person is out of town."

"Where did he go?"

"They didn't seem to know."

"Well, suppose you get some one to call again and press the matter."

Mr. Burgundy whispered to his young assistant. The latter hurried out.

The judge having taken his place on the bench, Mortimer proceeded with more witnesses, calling first Detective Lynch of the homicide squad. After the usual questions of record, Detective Lynch told his own story of finding the body. Some woman, who had not been identified, had called up the police station and notified them that there'd been a murder and had given the address.

"That silly girl," thought Martin, and wondered uneasily what had become of her. Women did not register very strongly with him, and especially true was this in the present moment of stress and preoccupation. Still, he remembered how pretty she had been in that dim light, and how scared. Poor kid! Clinging type, he added to himself discreetly. Well, he'd probably never see her again. She hadn't wanted money; she was just scared.

"So when the call was passed on to me," continued Detective Lynch, "I takes two men and I goes over, and there sure enough is the body."

"Exactly what time was this?"

"Around ten forty-five. Well, there he was in the dark, about six or eight feet inside the door, on his back with a bullet hole in his chest and something white crammed in his mouth. I felt him and he was stiff and cold. Then I called the coroner."

"And what did the coroner say?"

"Said he'd been killed by an explosive bullet—made by drilling out the nose—that exploded into fragments as soon as it entered his body, killing him instantly—and that he'd been dead between five and six hours."

"Which corresponds to the time the shot was heard by the occupants of the room below—say five thirty-three in the afternoon. Did you discover any other evidence?"

"I did—plenty. There was one revolver lying on the floor next to the body, and there was another, which the police records show belonged to the murdered man, on the floor behind him."

"Is this the first revolver that was beside the body?"

"Yes, sir. That's it. It was loaded and one shell had been fired."

"Were there any fingerprints on the gun?"

"Plenty. We had them photographed. They were made with greasy fingers."

"Was there any smell?"

"Yes, sir. A strong fishy smell."

"As of caviar, perhaps?"

"That's right."

"What caliber is this weapon?"

"Thoity-two, sir—same as the size of the bullet that went through the theater tickets in the pocket of Fortescue's dressing gown."

"Do you recognize this?"

"Sure thing. It's the letter found in the corpse's mouth."

The district attorney interrupted his cross-examination to place the revolver, the tickets and the letter in evidence.

It was during this pause that Mr. Burgundy's assistant returned quite breathless, wrote something on a piece of paper, and shoved it under Mr. Burgundy's nose. It read:

Van Leer left suddenly on receiving telephone call at about half past five on October 17th. Hasn't been heard from.

Mr. Burgundy shoved the note along to Martin.

"What do you make of that?" he whispered, indicating the date and hour.

Martin clasped his head. "Something—I don't know what."

"For Heaven's sake, man!"

"Don't get excited. It'll come to me," said Martin. "Keep in touch with that number. Call it every fifteen minutes. He'll probably read of the trial and show up. Subpoena him at once."

"If there's anything worth remembering you'd better be quick about it," whispered the lawyer. "But with what he's got on you, I can't see what good it'll do you." He turned and gave instructions to his assistant.

The district attorney had by this time finished with exhibits A, B, and C, and was resuming the cross-examination of the witness.

"Immediately upon finding the body what did you do?"

"I sent for the coroner. And while I was waiting for him to arrive we looked around. Detective Connerty reported there was a drunk two floors up. So up I went and I found——"

"One moment. Was the door of the upper room unlocked?"

"Yes, sir. It was half open. He must have been too drunk even to close it after him when he came up after killing——"

"One minute. These rooms were occupied by Mr. Martin Field,

were they not?"

"Yes, sir."

"Was Mr. Field at home?"

"Yes, sir. He was very much at home. He was completely ossi-
fied—I mean drunk."

"Describe how you found him."

"Well, there he was sunk down in a big chair, and cold—fairly
stinking with whisky."

"Were there any bottles and glasses?"

"Yes, a whole table full of them and some on the floor, empty
ones. And a silver prize mug, too, and a broken tumbler. The
whole place was a mess. Cigarette stubs——"

"One moment. Did you count the cigarette stubs?"

"I did. There were thirty-six."

"Thirty-six cigarettes. That's a good day's smoking. Was there
anything else?"

"Yes, sir. A small half-empty jar of caviar."

"That is very important. Did he have any of it on his person?"

"Yes, sir. He'd been eating it with his fingers; his right hand
was greasy with it."

Mortimer put two other detectives on the stand to corroborate
the testimony of Detective Lynch. Following these he called two
fingerprint experts who positively identified the fingerprints on
the revolver as Martin's.

Then the district attorney had the clerk read the letter which
had been found in the dead man's mouth. It was addressed to
Martin Field and had to do with a stock transaction. It was signed
by Creighton Fortescue, and was dated September 18th.

"That was just two weeks before the murder," explained
Mortimer, passing the letter to the jury. "And just two weeks
before the company went into bankruptcy. An investigation of
Martin Field's stock account shows that on September 20th he
purchased from Fortescue & Co. these ten thousand shares at the
price mentioned in this letter.

"The price of the stock, following the receivership, fell from
$52\frac{3}{4}$ to $12\frac{1}{4}$—a drop of $40\frac{1}{2}$ points—representing a money loss
to Martin Field of exactly a half million dollars. Even a man of
Martin Field's wealth could not but feel that he had let himself
be taken in rather ridiculously.

"Here, ladies and gentlemen of the jury, is the reason for the
murder. It was with this letter that Martin Field swore to choke
Creighton Fortescue. It was this very letter that was found in the
dead man's mouth. The prosecution rests!"

CHAPTER 12

STALLING FOR TIME

Only poisoned liquor could have produced the state of intoxication in which he was found.

MARTIN smiled a bit uneasily as Mr. Burgundy bent over to him, whispering: "Pretty quick work! Well, are you ready to have me go ahead?"

"Stall, if you can, till to-morrow," Martin told him. "You might say it looks like a put-up job. Something like that. Go ahead."

"Hm-m-m!" said Mr. Burgundy. "That's a good point." Then he took the floor, gravely consulted his watch, puffed out his chest and began:

"Your Honor, ladies and gentlemen of the jury: The sole contention of the defense to these cruel charges is that the defendant has no memory whatsoever of having killed Creighton Fortescue. He sits there, hearing the charges against himself, as innocent in his mind as any man can be who has no memory of an act.

"It is quite impossible to attempt any defense. The prisoner is helpless to defend himself against any charges, however cruel and unnatural, that his personal enemies may choose to bring against him; whether these be true or false, or even the perperation of some fantastic jest. For how easily might not a personal enemy have taken advantage of a man insensible from, let us say, doctored liquor, to have framed every bit of this exquisite evidence? It is all much too pat.

"The defendant is not a man whose courage comes by the pint. He is not a man to drink himself insensible. He is a man of courage and achievement, not a sot. Only poisoned liquor could have produced the state of intoxication in which he was found. For two whole days—forty-eight hours—he lay insensible. I feel sure that the testimony of such intoxication is not against the defendant."

Martin clapped his hand to his forehead. "My God!" he said aloud. And there flashed through his memory how he had poured the liquor into himself in vain effort to get drunk, and how, finally, he had taken only one swallow of gin and——"Good heavens!"

He heard Burgundy going on: "And I put the question: was Martin Field drugged or was he drunk? And I ask them, humane and intelligent, sensible grown-ups, would they have taken the affair at the club quite as seriously as the district attorney pretends to take it—who, it is to be remembered, was termed on that occasion a 'dumb ass' by the prisoner. Certainly the proposition to choke Creighton Fortescue with his own letter could not have been intended seriously. Figuratively, yes. But only a dumb ass could have believed——"

"Your Honor, I object."

"I trust that the stenographer will put quotation marks upon the epithet," said Burgundy.

"Proceed," directed the judge.

"That such a proposition was ever made with figurative intent," continued Mr. Burgundy, "might well have instigated what would appear to be a fiendish jest. Fortescue was murdered—by whom? I ask you, ladies and gentlemen of the jury, would Creighton Fortescue, who for two weeks following the affair at the club had maintained a bodyguard—would he have unlocked his door to the man who had sworn to kill him?"

"Good gosh!" exploded Martin, recognizing his own weak point.

Mr. Burgundy was doing himself credit. With as forlorn a case as this to defend one might have expected far less.

"Who, then, killed Fortescue? I'll answer that. Some woman he had ruined! Yes, probably some woman who, having lost all that life held most sacred to her, still retained her latchkey."

"Heavens!" exclaimed Martin, and this time he said it

aloud. For this was almost second sight on his lawyer's part.

"And having slain her seducer, she telephoned to the police and gave herself up—— Not a bit of it. She telephoned the other boy friend. There's always another. And there was plenty of time, from five thirty till ten forty-five. Together they framed the whole thing. They'll pin it on Martin Field. There he is just back from the woods, resting up. The rest is easily imagined. A few drops in a glass, the scene set and the evidence planted—the perfect frame-up."

A murmur of excitement swept over the courtroom. Mr. Burgundy puffed with self-appreciation. It was at this very moment that he decided to double his fee.

"Yes, the perfect frame-up. The mind that conceived it must have been well versed in criminal procedure. Your Honor, ladies and gentlemen of the jury, the defense has no defense against such an attack. Here are the revolver, the bullet-holed tickets, the letter—exhibits A, B, and C. The defense has but one exhibit - the epithet. 'Dumb ass.' "

"I object!" shouted Mortimer, his face livid.

"I don't wonder," returned Burgundy.

"Your Honor," said Mortimer, "these implications come very near to being direct accusation. I demand to know whether the defense intends to charge me directly with anything so inconceivable as this—with compounding murder and falsifying evidence!"

The judge rapped with his gavel. "The defense will answer that question," he said coldly.

Mr. Burgundy hesitated. He looked a little sheepish after his outburst.

"The defense is hardly prepared to go that far," he replied. "The defense merely adduces possibilities in the contention that the evidence might well have been falsified and that motive for such falsification might not have been lacking, as, for example, the epithet—always, of course, in polite quotation marks.

"I should like to ask the district attorney if, in all his years of practice in the criminal courts, he has ever seen a more perfect example of framing?"

Mortimer was instantly on his feet.

"I will answer that here and now," he said furiously. "A drunken man doesn't conceal his tracks. Martin Field's tracks were neither more nor less than would be expected of a man in his condition. I know a frame-up when I see it. There is not one least particular about this evidence that remotely suggests a frame-up. Does that answer you?"

Martin clapped his hand to his brow again. "Good God in heaven!" he exclaimed quite aloud.

"Very well," continued Mr. Burgundy. "I can only point out to the jury how tidily conclusive, how neatly convincing is the evidence. It's nothing if not pat. A valet could not more neatly have laid out a suit of clothes. The revolver, the letter—and that fishy fingerprint! Come now, nothing was ever as simple as all that. Are these the footprints made by a drunken man or are they patterns made with a stencil?"

He paused, aware that he was somehow carrying his point, aware, also, of some mysterious power of inspiration which made him be strangely apprehensive. Was he convincing himself? Or had he possibly stumbled upon the truth?

Every instinct of Mr. Burgundy was to avoid the truth. Never in all his professional career had he won a case on facts. Mr. Burgundy, virgin to all veracity, would have come upon the naked truth with the same flutter of the heart as an old maid finding a man under her bed.

Martin was smilingly unconcerned—and Mr. Burgundy was suspicious. He could smell a frame-up a mile away, and something distinctly of that aroma seemed to pervade the atmosphere. All that evidence so neatly laid out——

He looked at Martin again, and the virgin in him sensed that there was a naked truth under the bed.

"I object to all this," Mortimer here interposed. "It is for defense to adduce proof to disprove the evidence, not to impinge the honesty of the prosecution without due and properly documented grounds."

"Objection sustained," said the judge. "I do not feel that observations of such an intuitive nature and so primarily instinctive are pertinent. Unless the defense can adduce proper evidence to substantiate them, I shall have to rule that they be stricken from the record."

"On that point I shall have to ask an adjournment," said Mr. Burgundy. "It is well past four o'clock, anyway."

The judge immediately rose.

Mr. Burgundy had a great deal to say to Martin, but he began warily. What was Martin up to? There was something very strange behind that smile; something fishy.

"Well," he said, "how did you like my line about the frame-up?" And he fixed Martin with his most suspicious look.

"Swell," said Martin. "You've put him on record. You couldn't have done it better."

"So? You remember something, perhaps? With nothing between you and the electric chair, you sit there and smile. Monkey
business! Now what good is it to the defense that he should
go on record that the evidence was not framed?"

"It commits him. A man who has once committed himself is
in a delicate position. All you have to do now is to go ahead
and prove that it was all a frame-up. I think your premise was
excellent. You convinced me."

"Convinced you? Are you crazy? I might as well convince myself."

"Oh, then, you don't really think it was a frame-up?"

"Jumpin' Jupiter!" cried Mr. Burgundy, and raised his hands
to high heaven.

But Martin was unmoved. "What do you hear from Van Leer?"

"Yah! yah! This Van Leer. And what is it about this Van
Leer? I've had the young man from my office stop in at the
club and take a look at that pile of mail there. Mostly bills.
But there was a letter from the State Department; it was post-
marked the twentieth. So there you are. He got the telephone
call, and didn't wait for the letter. A consular job. Heaven knows
where. If you want I'll wire the State Department."

"Perhaps that's all it is, the call he was expecting." Martin
was careful. "You don't think that this sudden disappearance on
October 17th at exactly five-thirty o'clock has any significance?"

"Between you and me, no! It sounds fine, of course, but when
you analyze it, what does it amount to? How many people were
getting telephone calls at exactly five-thirty on October 17th?
How many persons were rushing for trains and going places—
disappearing, if you want to call it that?

"Van Leer was expecting a consular appointment, wasn't he?
His mother lives in Buenos Aires, isn't that what you told me?
And he was a sort of admirer of yours, if I judge rightly. So
there isn't anything very odd about his disappearance, except
that it happened to coincide with the murder. And I guess there
was reason enough for Mortimer not to have bothered with him
in the fact that he was your particular friend.

"But that doesn't mean I can't use it, and use it in a big way.
That's what I'm getting at. If I could only find out what's going
on in the back of your head. You've got me thinking there's a
frame-up somewhere. I can smell it!"

"Swell," said Martin. "Let's stick to our guns on that. I was
drugged and framed. All we need now is to prove it. That, of
course, I leave to you, Burgundy."

The lawyer spread his hands once more in despair.

"But there isn't any proof."

"Why not challenge Mortimer on the disappearance of Van Leer? Make a big issue of it. Make the State produce him at the State's expense. Hold the whole works up till it does."

Mr. Burgundy scratched his chin. After a moment he shook his head.

"Not too good," he said. "If Van Leer's disappearance has anything to do with you, it would be that the boy cleared out in order to keep from having to testify against you. You don't remember him dropping in on you that afternoon, do you? Suppose it's that? An eyewitness——"

"Yes, I suppose it would look that way," mused Martin. And he paced the floor. "Burgundy, we've got to hold the show up somehow. Do you suppose——" He stopped short in his tracks. "Holy cat! Here, give me that newspaper. Let's see what that stock did. Where the hell—— Bonds—stocks—curb. Here we are. Look, Burgundy, that damned stock is up eleven points!"

"You should have let me in on it," said Burgundy. "Eleven points is a good profit."

"Don't you realize that Account 3 X is just a fake; that the whole order was just a fake? Either some one in your office was the sucker, or Mortimer did have the line tapped. I didn't buy a share. The rest of the market's down. Some one bit. You weren't half careful enough. I warned you!"

"But he couldn't! It just isn't possible! I put that call through from my own house."

"Well, there you are. Mortimer was short of that stock. I happened to know that. I sent a fake order, and he rushed to cover. And a pretty penny his wire-tapping will cost him."

"So!" said Burgundy. "He's too smart, for once! But can you beat it? And I thought you were crazy!"

"I was right, wasn't I? And now that he has got stung, he may follow up that phone call and—— Well, let's not worry about that. You'll challenge the State to-morrow on Van Leer's disappearance and put it up to the State to produce him. We'll make an issue of it—just to see what happens. Then, if the boy never shows up at all, we'll go on from there."

"You mean that you'll pin it on Van Leer?" asked Mr. Burgundy incredulously and eyeing Martin with a dreadful suspicion.

"No, hardly that! That would be laying myself open to a charge of having done away with the boy in order to pin it on him. No one would believe it, anyway. Why should Van Leer have killed

Fortescue?"

"A girl, perhaps," said Burgundy. "You could easily pin it on him."

"Nothing like that, Burgundy. Not if I have to go to the chair. Van Leer is a decent young fellow. He could not have had anything to do with it. That sort of charge would only reflect on me. But suppose he has gone fishing and been drowned or, what is more likely at this season, has gone shooting and met with an accident?

"Great guns, I've had plenty of narrow escapes myself. An accident in the woods—they happen every day. A half-breed trapper was shot on my place the last time I was up there—not two miles from my own camp. I found him myself. A fellow can disappear in the woods so easily. He may have flown in and crashed.

"There's a possibility that Fred Van Leer might never show up. In which case, having claimed him as a material witness, we could hold the whole trial up indefinitely."

Mr. Burgundy considered this.

"Yah! If we could make out a case against Van Leer at the last moment like this—— But we'd have to make more of an issue of it than just that Mortomer hadn't called him. In fact, after our having bellyached for an immediate trial and crowded our case in on a busy session, we'd have to show good cause for the court to give us a postponement of as much as twenty-four hours. Certainly not more than that."

"That's not so hot, Burgundy," said Martin and resumed his pacing. "But even twenty-fours hours——"

The lawyer shook his head. "I'll give it a try. But take it from me, it will be short and sweet to-morrow. I'm leaving you the paper."

Twenty-seven hours! Something was holding up Chuck. There might have been difficulty in finding him, in spite of all the directions Martin had given Chuck. But it might also be that the matter was in the hands of the Canadian Mounted Police. Obviously one did not send stock orders to aviation fields. Suppose Mortimer had traced that call?

For Martin, this was the most difficult part of the whole business. What a lot of chances there were when you began to think about them in the middle of the night! An accident in the woods —like that trapper. Or a crashed plane. Remote contingencies. The barest chance. One in a thousand. But take a thousand such one-in-a-thousand chances and the bets were even.

Twenty-nine hours——twenty-eight hours——twenty-seven——

CHAPTER 13

MARTIN ADMITS—WHAT?

At Martin's burst of laughter, livid rage flared in Mortimer's eyes.

COURT opened with Mr. Burgundy resuming where he left off. "Your Honor," he began, "the defense has been required to substantiate its allegations that the defendant was framed! The defense does not present these allegations as allegations. It does not make a definite charge against any one of having planted false evidence. It merely presents a hypothesis, not to be proved beyond a reasonable possibility, that the case might have been framed against the prisoner. If there can exist such a hypothesis then the case against the prisoner is not proven."

The judge nodded. "Obviously, in the case of all circumstantial evidence. Proceed." His tone was short.

Mr. Burgundy, however, was never too easily put out.

"That an innocent man could have been drugged and this evidence rigged against him by some man who knew all about the affair at the club—who had, let us say, been actually present at the club on that famous occasion, who knew Martin Field quite well, but who was capable of trading upon this friendship to ruin him in order to save the woman who killed Fortescue—and instinct tells me that some woman killed him—that such a hypothesis is possible, then the case against Martin Field is not proven.

"Here, the prosecution says, is positive evidence. But it is not positive. It is anything but positive, because a more reasonable explanation can be adduced from the evidence than that the prisoner is guilty of this crime.

"I submit in substantiation of this statement a hypothesis and I submit it to this intelligent jury as the more probable story. First, because it is so much more the casual way things like this happen in real life. Second, because Martin Field could not have done it—not according to the hypothesis presented by the prosecution."

He paused and threw a glance at Martin, as much as to say, "This is just a stall." Then he went on.

"Why do I say a woman did it? Some instinct, perhaps, coupled with a few observations of such seeming inconsequence as to appear negligible. I do not believe Creighton Fortescue would have unlocked his door to Martin Field. Just that. Nothing as pat as a caviar fingerprint.

"If Creighton Fortescue unlocked his door to any one not of the hotel staff and well known to him, it must have been to a woman he was expecting. Or what is equally acceptable as a probability, the woman still had her latchkey.

"That is life, not testimony. Small things like that are subtle and convincing. In a frame-up you will always find all the big things pointing one way; all the little things will be pointing the other way. I submit that it is far easier to explain that caviar fingerprint and the letter crammed into the dead man's mouth than it is to explain the unlocking of that door.

"Let me prove that statement. I say that Martin Field has been framed. Who would or could have framed him so perfectly? And where is there any evidence that he was framed?"

Another pause.

"First, who could have done it? Some one who knew all about Martin Field's boast that he would get Fortescue; some one who had, as I say, been present at the club on that memorable afternoon; some one who was Martin Field's friend and who could have dropped in at his rooms for a drink.

"Secondly, who would have done it. Some young man yet in the first blind passion of youth, whose love for a woman would have blinded him to what he was doing to save her. Some one who would have rushed to her assistance the moment she called him on the telephone; some one who would have run away and hid his face.

"And last but not least, some one whom the prosecution would have conspicuously refrained from calling to the witness stand, though he had been not so much a witness as a principal in the affair at the club.

"Ladies and gentlemen of the jury, I present to your consideration a certain fact of deep significance. On Saturday the seventeenth of October, shortly after five-thirty o'clock in the afternoon, which is the very day, hour, and minute that Creighton Fortescue was foully murdered, one Frederick van Leer received a telephone message at the club, and rushed wildly thence and has since disappeared.

"Where is Frederick van Leer? Who called him to the telephone, and who subsequently called the police to notify them of the murder? Why did Frederick van Leer disappear? And why did the prosecution make no effort to subpœna him? All this reeks of caviar.

"Of course the defense offers no proof that Frederick van Leer framed Martin Field, his friend. It merely offers it as a hypothesis to show how easily the big clews, such as the letter in the dead man's mouth, can be explained away. But who will explain such a small thing as the unlocking of that door?

"Ladies and gentlemen of the jury, there is a locked door between the prosecution and any proof that Martin Field killed Creighton Fortescue!"

He paused upon this climax, his right hand upraised, perspiration upon his brow. A faint tremor ran through the court.

"I will now call the prisoner to the witness chair. And it will be the purpose of my examination to show that Martin Field has no memory whatsoever of killing Creighton Fortescue.

"First, how is it possible that a man could be so drunk as to have no memory of such an awful deed, and yet not so drunk but what he was able to perpetrate it?

"Second, he is a man helpless before these cruel charges—not only helpless, but of such fine courage and honor that he will not offer to defend himself. For he says that if it be true that he killed this man he is the first to demand that the law be carried out. If Martin Field remembered anything he would have pleaded guilty! But he remembers nothing."

Mr. Burgundy dabbed his bald spot with his handkerchief while Martin took the chair and was sworn in. He felt that he had done himself proud.

His secret of success in the law was not to be hampered by convictions. He always knew when he had the ground under his feet, which is to say when he was lying.

Here was Martin swearing to speak the truth, the whole **truth,** and nothing but the truth, which meant to Mr. Burgundy **that** probably everything that his client said would be false.

This thought gave Mr. Burgundy a great confidence. He began his cross-examination with a natural question.

"What was the last thing you remembered doing before, as **you** say, your memory became a blank?"

Martin rubbed his forehead. "It's hard to say."

"You probably remember flying back from Canada, **don't** you?"

"Yes, and I probably remember getting out of the plane at **the** flying field."

"Do you remember that?"

"Yes, but I can't be sure it was that particular time that I re-member getting out of the plane. You see, I've flown back **from** the woods and gotten out of the plane so often in just the same way."

"Where were you flying from?"

"From my place up in Quebec."

"And you say you probably remember flying down."

"I can't say I remember that particular trip as different or dis-tinguishable from any other."

"Do you remember being up in the woods?"

"Yes, that I do remember as a part of a certain train of events. And I remember it particularly for not having taken a gun in my hands the whole time I was there. Also I counted more moose than I'd ever seen before on any trip. And just before I left I found a poor half-breed who had either shot himself or been accidentally shot. I remember all that quite perfectly."

"You don't, however, remember leaving the flying field?"

"I do, and I don't. It might have been this time or another time. I confuse the occasion."

"When does your memory of consecutive events begin again?"

"It begins when I came to two days after the murder. Every-thing is perfectly clear from then on."

"You mean that everything in between is a blank?"

Martin did not answer at once. Instead he rubbed his forehead again.

"Not quite that. I vaguely remember something nightmarish that I can't remember. It's just like a tune that is running in my head, but I can't sing. Or it's like a name I'd know if somebody'd say it. It begins with K, no with B. I suppose I must have been

frightfully drunk. I hadn't had a drink for weeks. I never drink
when I'm out of the city."

"Say you don't remember killing Creighton Fortescue? You
don't remember cramming the letter into his mouth?"

Suddenly Martin leaned forward, his eyes closed.

"Yes, I remember—I remember——" He clasped his head in an
apparent agony of effort. "Letter—mouth—yes, I seem to remember that!" He beat his knuckles against his forehead. "Mouth
- letter——"

"Is that all that you remember?"

"I almost got it. Wait a minute."

Mr. Burgundy shook his head sadly and smiled as he turned to
Mortimer.

"Your witness."

Mortimer smilingly took the floor. He adjusted his gardenia
and straightened himself in his tight-fitting coat with the sleek
gesture of a cat. A small, dapper man, he stood in marked con-
trast to the bronzed and rugged Martin.

"Your Honor," he began, "we are not engaged here in proving the value of evidence as evidence, or in exercising our in-
genuity in devising pretty stories of what might have happened.
I asked that the defense make and substantiate a definite charge
that the evidence brought by the State had been deliberatly
falsified.

"This it has not done. The interesting deviation by the defense into the theory of pure evidence is nothing more than a
futile effort to impede the course of justice. I ask that all of it
be stricken from the record."

The judge pursed his lips. "The objection is well taken. There
are, however, points in the defense's argument that seem to the
court quite pertinent and admissible. The prosecution will proceed with the cross-examination of the witness."

Flushing at this rebuff, the district attorney faced the witness chair. The figure of Martin seated there gave him evident
satisfaction, for he stood a moment smiling sardonically, clicking his tongue and wagging his head pityingly. It was the sort
of dumb show that he had often used with great effect. But the
effect was lost on this occasion, because Martin suddenly laughed
out. It was all so sudden and spontaneous, that burst of laughter,
that even the judge was caught unprepared and forgot to rap.

Instantly all false pity was banished from Mortimer's face.
Livid rage flared in his eyes. His voice trembled a little as he
began:

"So you thought that all you had to do was to pretend that you'd forgotten all about it and you'd go free. Now, isn't that just too simple for words! I wonder nobody has been clever enough to think of it before. Not remembering puts a schoolgirl's complexion on murder. Don't you know that intoxication is no excuse, and that when a man gets drunk he takes upon himself the responsibility for anything he may do while drunk? Didn't you know that?"

"Yes, of course," said Martin. "But there is one exception."

"Oh, is there? Well, I suppose that anything that Martin Field does is the one exception. Is that what you think?"

Martin smiled. "The one exception is when a person is forcibly drugged with doctored liquor. I do not think any court would hold a man responsible then, do you?"

"So, you say that you were forcibly drugged?"

"No, I do not say that. I only say that I'm not at all sure my liquor was not doctored. I'd been away, you know, and it would have been quite easy to have done it. Perhaps you didn't know, Mortimer, that Fortescue was quite capable of doing it, and that when I said I'd get him there at the club, I was in deadly earnest, because I knew that, after what he'd done to me, if I didn't get him first he'd get me."

"Oh! So, you admit that you killed him in self-defense?"

"I do not. I have no memory whatsoever of killing him—if I did."

"But you admit your intention was to kill him?"

"Certainly."

"You premeditated this murder?"

"My dear fellow, it was a matter of the most infinite detail, preoccupying me for weeks."

CHAPTER 14

A WOMAN SPEAKS

"The hand that killed Creighton Fortescue is the hand that made those fingerprints!"

THE district attorney's mouth fell open. He could say nothing for a space of seconds. He merely stared incredulously at Martin, and Martin smilingly stared back.

"It is scarcely necessary to point out to the jury that this is a very important admission on your part. Such plotting and planning to kill rather discounts any excuse you might have adduced from the possibility of your liquor having been doctored. Now doesn't it?"

"Oh, absolutely! I had to get him before he got me. Whether the liquor was poisoned or not is just a fine point in another argument—an academic argument as to whether a drunken man is always responsible. It could hardly be used as a contention of self-defense, although it would bear out my statement that he was out to get me. I don't suppose you had that liquor analyzed, did you, Mortimer? I'd be interested. They tell me I was very near to passing out cold. Then we would not have had this beautiful trial, would we?"

The judge rapped severely at this.

"The witness will confine himself to answering the questions put to him by the district attorney."

Mortimer breathed a little easier at this, too. He was quite unused to cross-examinations in which the witness did the questioning. His customary method was to hector and confuse the witness. He hardly knew any other. But could such a method be applied to a man of Martin Field's desperate courage and utter sang-froid? Mortimer fingered his gardenia self-consciously.

"Aren't you old enough to know that that sort of twaddle won't go down in court? Doctored liquor! You started drinking because you were ashamed to show your face in town. You probably came straight from the plane to your rooms. You were going to wash up and then go over to the club for breakfast.

"Well, you hadn't the nerve. So you took a couple of drinks on an empty stomach to get your courage up. But you knew what a fool you'd look walking into the club, and you couldn't face it. So you had a few more drinks, and you even rummaged around for something to eat and dug up a jar of caviar. You were ashamed to call the restaurant or you were lying low for Fortescue.

"I don't know how you'd planned to get him—probably by poisoning *his* liquor. But by the time you'd had half a dozen drinks on nothing but caviar for breakfast and thirty-six cigarettes, and had brooded enough on the wrong he'd done you, or what a sucker you'd been, you forgot your pretty plans and went down and shot him—shot him in cold blood! Crazy drunk—cramming the letter in his mouth—leaving the revolver——

"And you have the nerve to pull this sort of blah about his poisoning your liquor! Self-defense? Did he come to your room to kill you or did you go to his room to kill him?"

"You are asking me to remember something I do not remember," replied Martin calmly.

"Why, if you were so afraid of him, didn't you go to the police?"

"How naive of you, Mortimer! What good are the police till after you've been murdered? I dare say that if I'd waited till Fortescue had got me, the police would have been right on the job. But where would I have been? I'd have missed all the fun."

"Fun!"

"Why, yes. Speaking for myself, of course. I don't know about you."

"Do you realize that you must go to the electric chair for this? Do you? Answer me!"

For reply Martin leaned back in the witness chair and regarded

Mortimer with his broadest smile.

The judge bent across his desk. "The witness will answer the questions put to him, and he will confine himself to answering."

"But what," asked Martin good-naturedly, "is the answer to a question like that?"

Mortimer put his question differently. "You know the penalty for murder, do you not?"

"Oh, yes!"

"Then you must know that having killed Creighton Fortescue——"

"I object," put in Mr. Burgundy.

The district attorney forced a laugh. "Well, if we must be so precise about it: you remember perfectly killing him. You remember planning the murder. You must know that the evidence against you is conclusive."

"I object."

"At least so conclusive that there can be no possibility of any verdict but guilty."

"I object."

"And such a verdict means death at the hand of the public executioner."

But no sooner had he spoken these last words than he realized his mistake.

"Public executioner—yes," repeated Martin as if inviting Mortimer to go on.

"Why, ladies and gentlemen of the jury, have these gray walls ever looked down on a more cold-blooded fiend than this!"

"No," responded Martin, looking at the walls.

"Oh, the prisoner is proud of it!"

Martin snapped to attention. "Which of us are you referring to?"

The judge rapped. Mortimer flushed and compressed his lips. Dangerous ground! It would be just like Martin to mention that last bet.

He reached for the letter, Exhibit C, and changing his entire tone of voice, said wearily, "Do you recognize this letter?"

"Yes."

"Is it the letter with which you swore to choke Creighton Fortescue?"

"It is."

"And it is the letter found in the dead man's mouth. Now this revolver: do you recognize this as being your revolver?"

"I could not say positively."

"Did you ever own a .32-caliber Police Positive Colt revolver?"
"I did once."
"Have you a license to own and carry a revolver?"
"No."
"Where did you keep this revolver?"
"I used to keep a similar revolver at my place up in Canada. I don't remember seeing it for years."
"So, you found it and brought it down with you?"
"No. I'm quite sure I didn't."
"But it might have been in your rooms?"
"Yes, very possibly. I've all sorts of hunting equipment. It might have been somewhere in my rooms. I haven't seen it for years."

"That admission is tantamount to a fact. It would seem that while putting away your shooting togs from your recent trip you happened upon it. For it must be your revolver. How else can you explain your very plainly marked fingerprint upon it?"

"Strange, isn't it?" said Martin.

Mortimer swung around at the jury. "Ladies and gentlemen of the jury, I offer this as conclusive evidence that the hand that fired the shot that killed Creighton Fortescue is the hand that made those fingerprints. And that hand is the hand of Martin Field!"

He paused now as if the whole matter wearied him. It was all too elementary. Martin's bravado and Lawyer Burgundy's innuendo had merely wasted the court's valuable time.

But there was another point; what was it the defense was trying to pull about that boy, Van Leer? Here he smiled a smile that fairly reflected Martin's, as he turned to him. He almost laughed.

"Now, what is all this about Van Leer having disappeared? He is—or was—a great friend and admirer of yours, wasn't he?"

"Why, yes," replied Martin, and the look in his eyes narrowed. "He is a friend of mine."

"You thought you could pin this on him, didn't you?"

"Certainly not."

"I'm not so sure of that. Why else should your counsel make so much of his being out of town? Is it not permissible for a young man to receive a last-minute invitation to a week-end? And suppose it had been something more important. You knew, did you not, that Van Leer was waiting for a consular appointment?"

"I did."

"And is it not also perfectly possible that he left town to avoid the disagreeable necessity of testifying against you? Had he happened in on you that afternoon you killed Fortescue, would——"

"Yes, I think he'd have left town."

"The prosecution respected Mr. Van Leer's feelings and saw no reason for putting him through the ordeal of appearing against his friend—the man he once so greatly admired. And when he hid himself in order not to have to look upon his fallen idol, you thought to make use of this disappearance to his discredit."

"That's a lie, Mortimer."

"You are trying to prove that he framed you."

"Good heavens, no! That was just an interesting idea of Mr. Burgundy's."

Mortimer passed his hand over his bald head in a dazed way.

"Well, I think that disposes of Mr. Van Leer's very mysterious disappearance."

"Yes, probably," said Martin queerly. And again he rubbed his forehead. "But there's something about him I can't quite get. Something nightmarish about a white black bear. If only I could remember."

"White black bear? Are you quite sure it wasn't a pink elephant?"

A light ripple of laughter rose from the room. It was Mortimer's first real score.

But Martin merely beat upon his brow. "I can't remember. I wonder if I could have sent the boy up to my place in the woods. But, no, he couldn't be there. I sent my customary code message to have all guests evacuated." And he studied Mortimer's face.

But the district attorney's face was impassive.

"Well, now, what was the other quibble?" Mortimer went on, smiling grimly as he drew his net tighter about his victim. "There was just one little thing, wasn't there? Oh, yes—the locked door. So you are sanguine enough to think that that little lock will save you from the electric chair? Your whole defense is now reduced to one little lock. This is pathetic. It is pitiful. You can ever answer why Creighton Fortescue so unwisely unlocked his door to you? Or who can say that the door was locked in the first place? Who——"

Suddenly a woman's voice cried from the back of the room:

"I can!"

CHAPTER 15

PERJURY!

Rough hands seized Martin and thrust him back to his seat.

AN INSTANT of breathless silence fell upon the courtroom, followed by a great stir as everybody stood up and turned about on creaking benches as the same trembling feminine voice repeated its startling statement, "I can."

Martin, from the vantage point of the witness chair, could see quite plainly the young woman standing up in one of the back seats. She was very still now and the attention of the whole room was focused upon her.

The judge rapped for order, and bending forward across his desk, said, "Have that person arrested."

Mr. Burgundy immediately stood forward.

"Your Honor, I claim this woman as a witness for the defense."

"Very well. Let her speak from the witness chair or not at all. The prosecution will proceed with the examination of the prisoner."

The district attorney smiled sourly. "I have finished with the witness. He may step down."

But Martin remained seated, watching Mr. Burgundy as he brought the girl forward. It was not till she was within the rail that he recognized her. "Good heavens! That Gretchen girl!"

Instantly he stood up; flung up his arms.

"You can't let this woman testify! She is just a hysterical girl. She wants to save me by confessing." And stepping down toward her, he said, "Gretchen, darling, get out of here. Don't you see how useless it is for you to do this?" Then he turned to the bench. "Your Honor, I protest against this woman being allowed to testify. She was to have been my wife. A wife cannot testify——"

At this point rough hands seized him and thrust him back to his seat behind the table. But he caught desperately at Burgundy and whispered, "For God's sake, stop her!"

But nothing could stop her. She turned lovely dark eyes on Martin for one long, yearning look and said:

"Thanks, Martin, darling, but this is my show from now on. Because I killed Creighton Fortescue. I won't say why I killed him, but I'll prove I killed him."

The judge rapped. "The defense called this woman as a witness. Will the defense, therefore, put the witness on the stand?"

Mr. Burgundy hesitated, looking first at Martin, then at the girl. Then everything was suddenly quite plain to Mr. Burgundy.

So, he *was* right, after all! A woman with a latchkey—and all that evidence neatly laid out to protect her. It was exactly as he had said. Well, now, it was all very noble and romantic of Martin Field to wish to die for love, but then that side of it was not Mr. Burgundy's business. His business was to defend the defendant—and Burgundy's reputation was tied up in it. So Mr. Burgundy turned his back on Martin and led the girl directly to the witness chair.

Martin was very well aware that Creighton Fortescue "knew" women. This unenviable reputation included, it seemed, an eye for real beauty, if there is such a thing. At least this young girl who stood now before him with her trembling hand on the book as she falteringly took the oath, had something that was very real; if it was not beauty it was equally appealing.

Martin leaned forward to look at her, remembering the while the frightened young thing that had clung to him that night in the dark. He was no lady's man, but he had known girls—society girls, show girls, working girls, native girls—but here was new wonder.

Never in his life had he seen the soul in a woman's eyes as he had seen it just now in her eyes as she had looked at him and said those first three words. "Thanks, Martin, darling." Of course, they did not know each other and the "Martin, darling" was pure bluff. But that look in her eyes——

And suddenly he told himself that he must have that—that nothing in life would ever be worth anything against that.

Then he heard Mr. Burgundy.

"Gretchen Demarest."

"Yes." Her voice was very faint.

"This is not, I take it, a bid for a night club contract. If you do not want the court to think that, I am afraid you will have to be a little more explicit. I will do my best to help you to make your confession in proper form. You will have to tell why you killed Creighton Fortescue. There must be a motive."

"I only said I could explain that locked door," she answered in a small, firm voice. "Well——" She put out her hand and something tinkled on the floor at Mr. Burgundy's feet.

He stooped and picked it up.

"So! Ladies and gentlemen of the jury, here at last is the latchkey; no longer a hypothetical latchkey, but the latchkey itself. That door is no longer locked. The way to the truth is open!

"This latchkey unlocks the motive for the murder. It unlocks the smile on the prisoner's lips. For now, also, it becomes clear that all this neatly laid-out evidence was indeed a frame-up. Only it turns out that Martin Field framed himself. He did it to save the woman he loves, the woman whom Creighton Fortescue had wronged, the woman who killed Creighton Fortescue to avenge her dishonor in the eyes of the man she loved. How tragically beautiful! You admit all this, don't you?" he asked the witness with perfect assurance.

She closed her eyes and smiled faintly. "I only know that he didn't kill Creighton Fortescue, because I killed him."

"I think, ladies and gentlemen of the jury, we are now getting to the bottom of this. I will put a hypothetical question to the witness:

"Is it not true that when Martin Field discovered that Creighton Fortescue had been before him in possessing you, he became so enraged that he cast you off, swearing that he would kill him?

"And is it not true that, in order to prevent Martin Field from committing this fatal act, you took it upon yourself to avenge your own dishonor?

"Is it not also true that, having done so, you lost your nerve and went to Martin Field, and that he was loyal and loving enough to make this heroic attempt to save you; and did he not

send you away and demand an immediate trial, pleading
nolo contendere and smiling in the hope of being convicted for
your sake?"

She made no answer. She only put up her hands to her face.

A sigh went up from the entire courtroom. Here was Drama,
Drama with a capital D. Tears trembled on the lashes of the
sentimental. The judge looked more myopic than usual.

Martin himself was moved. A silly emotion choked him in the
midst of an almost irresistible impulse to laugh out. Could anything beat old Burgundy! Burgundy the romantic! One plausible
story after another, just like that.

But what extraordinary intuition! All that about the locked
door the one kink in Martin's plot, the one point that he would
have had difficulty in explaining had the prosecution pressed it.
Then the woman, the latchkey, the planted evidence! Old Burgundy must have second sight! And he was probably right about
that liquor, too! Martin was beginning to be convinced that it
had been doctored. That gin——

And now, before his incredulous eyes, this lovely girl was offering her life to save his. Absurd! Preposterous! Another
Burgundy romance. Women were always trying it, either for publicity or out of hysterical impulse.

But had any one ever slipped through with a spurious confession? Could this girl possibly think that she could get away
with it? She would probably only ruin everything for him, but
at least he knew——Oh, wonderful absurdity!—that she was
sincere, that she was actually offering her life.

What was his life against such an offering as that?

He had no idea now what his chances were. All his deep-laid
plans were shot to pieces. Mortimer might get him or not. Nothing mattered; nothing at all but that girl sitting there, and the
look she had given him.

Suddenly he was on his feet. No one stopped him as he moved
across the small open space of floor. He encountered Mortimer,
but the district attorney merely stepped aside.

Martin laid fingers of steel on Burgundy's arm. Then he was
in front of the girl and she put down her hands and looked at him
again. Silence fell upon the courtroom. Martin had the feeling
that he and she were on a tiny islet in the midst of a vast sea of
silence.

Thus he stood for a long moment in front of her before he said
in a low voice, "Gretchen, darling!" and shook his head.

Then he smiled up at the bench.

"Your Honor, may I ask permission under these extraordinary circumstances, to act as my own counsel? Some twenty years ago I passed my law examinations and was admitted to the bar, but have never practiced."

The judge frowned, nodded.

"Very well, then, the defense asks that all this romantic nonsense be stricken from the testimony. In China, perhaps, one person may barter his life for another's, but not here. As for taking this confession seriously, I see that the district attorney smiles. The defense thanks the witness and asks her to step down."

"One moment," interposed Mortimer suavely. "I should, nevertheless, like to ask the witness a few simple questions."

Martin looked from the girl to Mortimer; his eyes pleaded mercy.

"Your witness."

Mortimer must have felt the hostility that breathed upon him from all sides. He began not too savagely.

"Where were you on October 17th at five-thirty o'clock?"

"I was——" She hesitated. "Why, I was in his rooms, of course."

"Whose rooms?"

"Mr. Fortescue's. If you mean at the time the shot was fired that killed him. I had to be there to fire it."

"You were with Creighton Fortescue, your former lover, because you thought that Martin Field, your present boy friend, was out of town. Is that it?"

A faltering, "Yes."

"Was it, perhaps, to return this latchkey, and just possibly to plead with Mr. Fortescue against his betraying to Mr. Field some secret of that earlier relationship—was it for some such reason that you went to his room that afternoon?"

Again the faltering affirmation.

"It must have been very awkward having your two lovers living so close together—only two floors apart."

"Yes, but that is how I met Martin."

"Then Mr. Field must have known about your earlier relations with Mr. Fortescue?"

"He did."

"But there was some little detail you were bent on hiding?"

"No. He knows everything. I wouldn't hide anything."

She cried this so passionately that Mortimer quickly dropped that attack.

"So you were in Creighton Fortescue's room when Martin Field shot him?"

"No, I wasn't—I mean he didn't. *I* shot him."

"But you used Martin Field's revolver?"

"Ye-s."

"And the revolver was in Canada—lost, if I remember correctly."

But he did not trap her so easily. She sat forward.

"No. I'd taken it. I found it in Martin's room."

"Just where in his room did you find it?"

A look of fear came over her face. She had, Martin felt certain, never been in his rooms. But apparently she was equal to the emergency. Martin's apartment being directly above would probably have had the same arrangement of rooms as Fortescue's.

"It was on the shelf in the little closet at the turn in the passage," she said. "It was tied up in some old hunting togs."

Martin tried to remember. He felt vaguely sure that there were some old shooting clothes in that closet. But the revolver he had kept in his desk drawer.

"So at least we have definite proof now that Martin Field kept a revolver in his rooms. The rest is, of course, perjury to shield him. I think, ladies and gentlemen of the jury, that we can now finally explain the unlocking of that closed door. I will ask the witness a hypothetical question:

"Is it or is it not true that, while you were in Creighton Fortescue's rooms, and being convinced of the fact that Martin Field was out of town, you yourself unguardedly opened the door that Fortescue himself would *not* have opened, and, in so doing, admitted Martin Field who had unexpectedly returned from the woods and who, finding you in this other man's rooms, shot and killed his rival? Is this the truth? Or will you persist in your silly lie about having killed him yourself?"

"I object," said Martin. "I object to the form of this question. I object that it is unnecessarily brutal. This is no common lie she is telling. It is an act of supreme courage."

"I ask your pardon," said Mortimer with sarcasm. "In such cases one looks to find less supreme courage than a common love of notoriety, or an ambition to appear on the stage. It is surprising that we have not had more confessions. You will probably mention this brave girl in your will—so soon to be probated. Well, young woman, is that your game?"

She bit her lips. "He couldn't——Oh, he couldn't think that!"

"Such an old game!" sneered the district attorney. "Why, it

is quite possible that you had never seen him before you came into this court. It might have just popped into your pretty head as you sat back there that all you had to do was to stand up and confess, and then go straight out to Hollywood. How long have you actually known Martin Field?"

"I—I don't—quite remember."

"Come, now, we've had enough of this loss of memory stuff. If you can't remember when you met him, it must have been a great many years ago."

"Yes."

"How long have you lived in New York City?"

"About ten months."

"You're not a very good liar, are you? You say you have known Martin Field for many years, and yet you testified a few minutes ago that you happened to meet him through his having rooms above Fortescue's. And you have only been in New York City ten months. I would just draw your attention to this inconsistency in order to make you see how tiresome this sort of perjury is. But, let us go on. You must remember the occasion of that meeting. What season of the year was it?"

"I think it was winter," she answered, terrified.

Mortimer laughed. "You realize that all this is perjury. You are under oath. Martin Field was in East Africa all last winter."

"I didn't offer to answer these questions. I only offered to tell the court how that door was opened. Some things are sacred."

"Sacred! My dear young woman, to call your love life sacred is to put brimstone on the altar. You were Creighton Fortescue's mistress, by the proof of that latchkey. A common prostitute, quick to sell out one rich lover for a richer one."

"I object!" cried Martin, clenching his fists.

"Well, now, tell the court how long you had known Creighton Fortescue."

"Ten months."

"Oh, then it was he who brought you to New York?"

"No, we met on the train."

"And before you got to New York he had given you a latchkey and you thought it was a wedding ring."

"To put it brutally—yes. I was very innocent."

"It is quite probable that you never knew Creighton Fortescue, either. Are you prepared to swear that this is a key to his apartment? You have taken quite a lot of the court's time already. I wouldn't impose any further if I were you."

"That key is to his apartment. I was his mistress."

CHAPTER 16

NEW DEVELOPMENTS

"I went all over the apartment."

MORTIMER yielded the point adroitly, a faint, grim smile at the corners of his lips. He paused for a moment to permit the girl's admission to have its effect on the courtroom. Then he continued his examination.

"Then we can say for sure that you knew Fortescue intimately. You were with him in some sacred intimacy on that afternoon of October 17th, at five-thirty."

"I was in his apartment—yes."

"What was he doing?"

"He was typing a letter."

Her voice as she said this became more assured.

"So when some one knocked at the door, it was you who went to open it?"

She hesitated and replied firmly, "No."

"You say he was typing."

"Yes. I heard him through the door. That is how he didn't hear me slip the latchkey in the lock when I let myself in. He jumped up, startled. He had a little nickel-plated revolver. I don't remember what I said—something about bringing him back his key. But

I meant to kill him. I had the gun wound up in a fur piece. He came at me. There must have been a window open. The door behind me slammed suddenly. I didn't hear the pistol go off. I just saw him look funny and go down."

"Then what did you do?"

"I don't know."

"You ran upstairs to Martin Field—to return him his revolver, of course."

"Yes, but not right away. I was rather dazed. I must have remained in the room a long time."

"And then you went up to Mr. Field's rooms?"

"Yes."

"But you have already testified that you were in Mr. Fortescue's apartment, believing Mr. Field was out of town. What made you think he would be up in his rooms?"

"I didn't think so. It just happened that he had returned."

"Oh, I see. He, too, had given you a latchkey."

"Yes," she said, and covered her face.

"Well, this is splendid! Your lies are a transparent cellophane wrapping for this exceedingly valuable bit of testimony. You testify that Martin Field was in his rooms. Do you realize that that testimony alone would be enough to send him to the chair?"

"Oh, no!" Her face now betrayed the agony of her panic. "No, he wasn't! I *am* lying."

"My dear girl, everybody knows that. You wanted to help this romantic-looking gentleman, whom you'd never seen till you came into this courtroom to pass an idle morning. You didn't want to harm him. Well, it's not too late. The veriest nitwit can see you're lying. Come, now, admit you've been making the whole thing up."

Tortured, still she had courage. She sat up very straight, gripping the arms of the witness chair.

"It's true. It's all true—except knowing Martin Field. I didn't know him. I'd never even met him. Are you satisfied?"

"Well, well! You are very confusing." Mortimer laughed and twiddled his gardenia.

"I can explain. After a time—I suppose it was only minutes—I began to realize what I'd done. I became terrified. Instinctively, I started to get away. I opened the door and there he was—Mr. Field. You're right about one thing. He *was* drunk. I'd never seen him before. He was standing just outside the door. When I opened it so quickly, he almost fell into the room.

"Well, there he was, and there was Creighton dead on the floor. I gave myself up. But then he said, 'Zish wazh my job' and patted me on the shoulder. Then he told me to get out quick."

Mortimer listened attentively and then he laughed.

"Tell me, did you put his revolver back on the shelf of the closet where you found it? Or wasn't there any revolver?"

"Yes—no. That's true, too."

A sound like laughing moved over the silence of the courtroom. Gretchen Demarest's face became a white mask of misery. She cast agonized looks at Martin, and the courage and the pity of her hurt him. He wanted to say something, but he could only look into her agonized eyes. If only he had known how to return that look she had earlier given him. He was, in fact, returning it now.

The color suddenly came flooding back into her cheeks; she even smiled faintly.

"No, I'd never known him. But I'd been up in his rooms," she said. And the tone of her voice carried a mysterious conviction.

She put her hands up to her face for an instant, lowered them and looked straight at Martin.

"Creighton made me. He had a key. A boy from his office named Benny made it. Creighton knew that Martin Field was away and he wanted to find out if he had left any clew on his desk as to where he'd gone. Everybody was trying to find that out. But there wasn't a thing.

"I went all over the apartment, and it was so different from other places. There were only men's things—guns, fishing rods, old boots, pipes. There wasn't a woman's slipper under the bed. Not even a woman's photograph in the whole place. There were books. I remember there was a book on Africa by his bed. I smelled his pillow. It wasn't perfume; it smelled only of tobacco —a nice man's smell. Well—I found the revolver, but I left it. Oh, Martin——"

He answered her with a smile, and she went on.

"About that liquor. Creighton said that Mr. Field had something special. He made me look. I could find only a few bottles. I brought down two that had been opened. Creighton went into the bathroom for a glass. Then he came out and said it was awful stuff and for me to take it right back. So I did.

"And after I left Creighton that afternoon, I went back again to Mr. Field's rooms. I'd left the door on the latch.

"I stayed there a long, long time, just looking at his things, and touching and smelling them. It was then that I began to see that I couldn't go on living with Creighton any more. And I couldn't hope to live with any one else after what I'd been—after

what he'd made me. I was done for. I was ashamed to even be in
that room. I felt that I was desecrating it. I just might as well
take the revolver down off the shelf. I did, and put it in my purse.
But when I got home with it I had a crying spell, and after that
I thought and thought.

"I went to sleep and had a nightmare. I dreamed that Creighton
had gone up to Mr. Field's room to kill him, and that Mr. Field
was looking for his revolver to defend himself.

"I woke up, realizing that it could very easily happen just like
that and that the first thing for me to do was to take the gun
back. Then I had another idea. I'd shoot Creighton, and then kill
myself. That's what I meant to do. It would have saved Martin.
If only I hadn't lost my nerve——

"Oh, Martin, I didn't know about the liquor! It never occurred
to me he would have done anything to it."

"My God!" said Martin aloud.

So old Burgundy was right about the liquor, too! That was a
close break. If I'd started in on the gin—— As it was, just that
one swig and I was out cold for two days. But could she be making this part up, too? That book on Africa by my bed? No, *she's
telling the truth!*

Mr. Burgundy, standing at Martin's elbow, also scented the
truth and instantly took alarm.

"I object!" he exclaimed. "I object to my client conducting his
own defense. It is my duty to defend him, to prevent him from
sacrificing himself to save this woman, and to prevent him from
obstructing justice and compounding a horrible crime."

The judge adjusted his glasses.

"The prisoner will be seated. The prosecution will continue."

Martin was dragged back to his seat behind the table.

Mortimer smiled a sickly smile. He paused for a moment while
he read a slip of paper which one of his assistants had thrust into
his hand. It concerned some matter of importance, but which for
the moment had lost all importance. With a preoccupied nod to
the assistant, Mortimer thrust the paper in his pocket. Then he
went on with his cross-examination.

"How, then, did you come to know Creighton Fortescue?"

"I told you the truth about that. And I don't think it matters
much now."

"Perhaps not. But it does matter when Martin Field asked you
to marry him. You will have to answer that."

He had the girl cringing again as he stood over her. She shrank back in the big chair, looking very small in it. But terrified as she was, she, nevertheless, defied him with her silence.

"You see," continued Mortimer, "your whole pretty little fiction again falls quite to pieces unless you can answer that question. You never actually knew Martin Field until after you had killed Fortescue—not till you opened the door to him, and yet—— Will the stenographer please read what Martin Field said when this witness first came to the witness chair."

After some minutes the stenographer found the passage and read:

"Gretchen, darling, for God's sake get out of here. Don't you see how useless it is for you to do this? Your Honor, I protest again this woman being allowed to testify. She was to have been my wife. A wife cannot testify."

"Yes," said the district attorney, "that is it. Practically his wife. Well, that does not check with your account of never having met him before the murder does it? Trying to pretend you don't know each other like any two crooks.

"Come, now, if you must have a share in it, admit that you've been months cooking this whole thing up together. And, of course, your exploration of an unknown gentleman's apartment, while it makes a good story, is equally fictitious.

"I compliment you on your histrionic abilities. You will, indeed, go far in Hollywood. But you won't get anywhere in a real court of law."

"I will answer that for you," she said interrupting him.

"Oh, let us hear some more romance!"

"I said that when I opened the door to run away, Mr. Field was standing just outside it. Well, that was not just a few minutes after I had killed Creighton—it was hours. It must have been near ten o'clock.

"When I saw him, I didn't try to run away. I wanted to be near him for just a few minutes. I wanted him to see me and speak to me, and I wanted him to know that I'd done it to save him.

"He told me to get out, but I wouldn't go—because it meant I would never see him again. I had made up my mind to go straight out and jump off the Queensboro Bridge.

"I said he was drunk. Yes, of course, he was drunk. But he was so gentle, so kind! I lost all my nerve. I began crying and saying I had nothing to live for and no place to go.

"That's when he asked me. He said he wanted to repay me for

saving his life, and that he'd give me everything in life to live for, beginning with himself if I wanted him. Drunk!" She covered her face with her hands.

One of the lady jurors gave an audible sob.

That was too much for Mortimer. He flung about facing the jury.

"Can it be that any one in his right mind believes this? What a web of contradictions! This proposal of marriage from the drunken defendant is represented as having taken place during that period in which the prisoner's mind is most completely blank.

"He had never met this woman before the meeting she describes. And I can assure you no woman has had access to him since his arrest. Yet he remembered her well enough to know her the moment she stepped forward. He called her by her first name. He even remembered having asked her to marry him—the kind of thing a man is most unlikely to remember under the most ordinary circumstances. This is valuable testimony for the State.

"If Martin Field remembers this meeting as she has described it, then he must remember everything that he professes to have forgotten. It is obvious that his lapse of memory is but a crude effort at pretense."

"I object!" cried Mr. Burgundy, finding the truth more than usually repellent. He had sensed all along that Martin Field was lying about his lapse of memory. To be sure, drunks did forget like that—and, Heaven knows, Martin had been drunk. But Mr. Burgundy's instinct had warned him. He felt that he had known all along.

"Very well." Mortimer swung about to Martin. "Not to remember is, of course, the commonest legitimate method of evading an answer."

"If I may speak," he said solemnly, "certain things *have* come back to me, and are rapidly coming back to me, although disconnectedly. For one thing, I remember putting the letter in Fortescue's mouth. I definitely remember that now. And I definitely remember asking this girl to marry me—and I wasn't to very drunk, either. Also, I remember there was a white black bear— or was it a bearskin rug? I think that if I could get a little bit drunk I'd remember everything perfectly. That probably wouldn't be allowed, would it? Pardon my suggesting it." He sat down.

Once more a stir of laughter. Even the judge smiled as he rapped for order.

Mortimer stood waiting till there was again silence—that tense silence Townsend would have said precluded catastrophe. He turned again to the girl in the witness chair.

"You killed Creighton Fortescue at five-thirty-two p. m. Now you say that you remained in the room with your dead lover for five hours."

"Yes."

"What did you do all that time—read a book on Africa?"

"I don't remember."

"You closed the window, didn't you?"

"Perhaps. I suppose I did."

"Did you take a nice hot bath?"

"No."

"Did you run a bath?"

"No."

"Did you shut off the water?"

"No."

"When the police arrived on the scene at ten-thirty that night there was a tub nearly full of water, still warm. Who ran the bath?"

"I suppose Creighton did."

"Wasn't he running that bath when you came in?"

"I—I don't remember."

Mortimer studied her silently for half a minute, during which her terror seemed to come back. He stood before her like an agile fencer watching for an opportunity to skewer his adversary.

"I have a deposition," he said at last, "made by the occupants of the room below that the sound of the shot was partly obscured by the noise of a running bath."

"Yes, perhaps. I don't remember. I suppose I must have shut it off. What difference does it make?"

"Oh, lots of difference. Well, now, you closed the window and you shut off the water in the bathtub. Then what? Did you take a nap?"

She drew a long breath and her small hands gripped the arms of the witness chair. Her voice was tense.

"I thought and thought about what I'd done and—and about killing myself. But I just couldn't. It was easier to wait for the police to come and get me. I thought about telephoning them."

"You did later."

"No."

"You didn't telephone and nobody came?"

"No."

"If some one had knocked, would you have let them in?"

"I don't know. But nobody knocked."

"Yes; nobody——"

"A telegram was delivered at Fortescue's room at six-thirty. The bell boy knocked several times and even tried the door, which rather proves that you weren't in the room at all. As a matter of fact, I doubt if you were within a hundred miles of the room.

"I would say that you were somewhere that Martin Field had taken you and was keeping you. He'd taken you away with him. And then something you told him made him leave you and come back to kill your former lover. You drove him to commit murder; you were responsible. Yes, quite so. But you did not fire the shot that killed Fortescue. You were not around." And Mortimer laughed.

"I *was* there! I must have been too dazed to hear the boy knock."

"You must have been quite unconscious."

"Yes. I fainted—I must have. I remember how suddenly it was night." She smiled weakly. It was evident, however, that she was clutching at straws.

"And when you revived, you found yourself still walking around touching and smelling things?"

"Yes—no, I was on the couch."

"And you didn't realize that you'd lost consciousness."

"How could I be conscious of being unconscious. I only remember that it was suddenly dark."

Mortimer sighed. "I am giving you every chance to prove that you killed Creighton Fortescue, but I can't even prove that you were within a hundred miles of him when he was killed. You were unfortunately unconscious when the boy knocked at the door. And you missed the opportunity I gave about the bath. Even that would have been something. He was about to take a bath. Instead, you say he was typing."

"Yes." Suddenly she leaned forward. "I can even tell you what he was typing, if that will satisfy you. I read it. Creighton always typed his love letters. But this was about collecting some money. It wasn't addressed to any one. It started: 'The man at the garage will tell you where you can get the money. But there's nothing in the newspapers yet. You'll have to wait till I see it in print. That was our arrangement. I am going to Palm——' It ended there. I read it about a hundred times trying to think who the girl was and what it all meant. And I added the word 'Beach' myself."

Suddenly Martin Field stood up behind the table.

"In all probability Frederick van Leer has been murdered," he announced in a cold voice.

CHAPTER 17

SURPRISE WITNESS

The judge was pounding with his gavel above the confusion.

THE words echoed through the still courtroom. They were followed by an interval of silence like that of held breath, as Townsend, would have said. Then confusion.

Rough hands seized Martin and dragged him down. But he broke away from them. He was on his feet again. The judge was pounding with his gavel. The clerk called, "Silence in the court!"

The judge spoke. "The court instructs the district attorney to take the immediate deposition of the defendant in such matters as concern the possible murder of Frederick van Leer. His disappearance was among the first points adduced by the defense. If the defendant has any proof that this Van Leer has met with foul play, it is important that such information be given to the police at the earliest possible moment."

At this Martin thrust himself out into the small open space of floor.

"It's as clear as daylight. Fortescue must have got him. There's no other explanation why Van Leer isn't here. I remember almost everything now. It's all coming back to me. I didn't kill Fortescue—I only meant to kill him. Van Leer had nothing to do with it, either. I'd sent him up to my place in the woods to get an albino black bear. Do you remember I said a half-breed trapper had been accidentally shot? Accidentally? I found him right near my camp in a little rocky place where I used to sit and smoke my pipe. Now does that letter make sense? Where is it, Mortimer? What did you do with it?"

Mortimer glared at Martin without answering. Then, turning to his assistant, he made a slight motion of his head. The assistant immediately stepped forward with a brief case. The district attorney opened it with slow deliberation. He took out a sheet of typewriter paper with a few sentences typed in the middle of it.

Martin snatched it impatiently.

"That telegram you said was delivered. Let's have that, too. It may be important. Now, listen to this."

He read from the typed sheet.

"The man at the garage will explain where the money will be. But there is nothing as yet in the papers and I am waiting till I see it in print as we arranged----"

"Your Honor, this is not written to a woman who is blackmailing him; it is written to the man he has hired to go up to my place in the woods and kill me. Payment to be made strictly C. O. D. The fellow has claimed his money for having killed that trapper, but Fortescue won't pay until he sees my name in the papers. Is it clear now? Perhaps the telegram has something to do with it. Let's see."

"THE LAUGH IS ON ME STOP BETTER LUCK NEXT TIME STOP HOLD THAT DOUGH   BENNY"

Martin laid aside the telegram, again addressed the judge.

"There you are! Benny—wasn't that the boy who made the pass-key to my room? Well, Benny has found out that it wasn't me he'd got and has gone back for another shot. And now he has probably got Van Leer, because as I said on the stand, I'd begun to think Van Leer might be up at my place and I'd sent my usual code message to evacuate all guests. If he isn't here it's because he's been done in."

"Your Honor," said Mortimer with his sneering smile, "I think that this fine example of inductive theorizing fairly completes the deposition. No one but the man who had himself composed it could so readily have interpreted these few sentences here.

"Quite obviously Creighton Fortescue was not typing, but was preparing to bathe at the time he was murdered. And the man who shot him wrote this message on the typewriter in order to explain the death of Frederick van Leer whose sudden disappearance had been part of the plot.

"In other words, when Martin Field sent the boy up to his place in the woods it was tantamount to taking him for a ride with the intention of pinning the crime on him. It was, indeed, all a gigantic frameup, as the defense has pointed out. The only slight miscalculation happens to be that, having killed Fortescue, he failed to dispose of his friend Van Leer.

"I may now set his conscience, if he has one, and the concern of the court at rest. Frederick van Leer has not been murdered. The State has been holding him under subpœna since——"

He paused and consulted the slip of paper that he had recently stuffed in his pocket.

"—since nine-thirty this morning. He will appear as a rebuttal witness."

Upon the consternation that followed this statement, the district attorney smiled while he adjusted his gardenia.

"Now, if I may be permitted to proceed with the trial of Martin Field for the brutal murder of Creighton Fortescue," he went on with sarcasm, "which, if my own memory does not fail me, is the case before this court——"

The district attorney turned now suddenly toward the witness chair.

"Why, my poor, dear, little girl—we'd forgotten all about you." Then in a tone of bitterest sarcasm, "I'm extremely sorry, but the State will have to hold you as an accomplice in this murder. It seems very plain now that you sold out Fortescue to Martin Field. You were the Lady Iscariot who opened the door to him. I arrest this woman on her own confession."

Martin gasped. Strong hands were drawing him back to his seat behind the table. He wanted to speak, to protest. They should not touch her. A sudden impassioned instinct possessed him to have her at his own expense. He had only to cry out, "She had nothing to do with it. I killed him. I'll prove it."

But even as he opened his mouth to speak that strange presence of mind in moments of emergency saved him.

He had a much better idea.

Mr. Burgundy was speaking; in fact, it appeared that Mr. Burgundy had been speaking for some minutes.

"The defense asks for a new trial."

"Petition denied," said the judge sharply.

Mr. Burgundy waved his arms. "Well, then, the defense accuses the prosecution of unethical practice with regards to evidence and witnesses. What right has the State to conceal important letters and telegrams? What right has it to—to *kidnap* witnesses?"

Mortimer was on his feet at once.

"I object! The matter was all of record in the inquest. Mr. van Leer is not kidnapped, much less murdered. He is, in fact, present in this court—and has been for some minutes."

"Oh!" gasped Mr. Burgundy, taken aback.

There was a stir in the back of the courtroom as Van Leer stood up.

He was noticeably pale, wore his right arm in a sling and was badly in need of a hair cut.

"Suppose you come forward," said the counsel for the defense. The courtroom being pack-jammed, this proved to be a difficult process, for Van Leer seemed very ill and weak, and barely able to walk. He required two policemen to assist him and to make a way for him.

One look at him and Mr. Burgundy saw the whole thing clearly. It was as he had earlier suspected, this Van Leer boy had blundered in on Martin at the awkward moment when he was killing Fortescue.

There was only one thing to do with an eyewitness. So Martin had given him a slug of doctored liquor and had shipped him off to the woods. Taken him for a ride.

But the boy had somehow escaped. Martin had suspected as much because there had be no notice in the papers. And so he had anxiously watched for him in order to subpœna and silence him, or at least to keep him out of Mortimer's hands.

There it was. Well, it was too late now.

No use now to ask for time to prepare the witness. Van Leer was a witness for the State. With a despairing gesture of spread hands, he turned toward his client.

"What now?" said the lawyer in a dispirited whisper.

But Martin was excited. "It's all come back to me, every damn thing. Just ask him—ask when—— No, never mind what you ask him. Ask him anything."

Mr. Burgundy was equal to most occasions, but he seemed a little bit at a loss now. He said perfunctorily:

"Mr. van Leer will take the witness chair."

CHAPTER 18

SOMETHING FISHY

"They tried to kill me—that's all!" replied **Van Leer**.

THE boy was so weak that he had to be half-lifted to the witness chair. He stood for a moment to take the oath, raising his left hand in lieu of the right which was in a sling.

"Your name?"

"Frederick van Leer."

"Age?"

"Twenty-five."

For a moment the boy seemed about to faint. Mr. Burgundy stepped forward and laid a hand on his shoulder.

"Take it **easy**, young man. You appear to have met with an accident."

"They tried to kill me—that's all."

"How did that happen?"

"They got me up in the woods," replied Van Leer, anger reviving him. "It was supposed to be an accident, of course, like those which so often happen. He had a half-breed killed two weeks before, just to make it seem more of a commonplace occurrence. I——"

"Not so fast," hastily interposed the counsel for the defense.

"I think you are voicing a highly prejudiced point of view—the one just now presented by the district attorney, which is all pure poppycock. Now, when did you get back, and from where?"

"From Martin Field's place up in Quebec Province. I got back this morning. I've been——"

"Confine yourself to answering my questions. You got in this morning—at what hour?"

"About nine o'clock."

"And were immediately subpœnaed?"

"Yes. And that was the first I knew of any of this. I've been kept prisoner."

"Not so fast. We'll come to all that. So you hadn't seen yesterday's evening paper, or this morning's?"

"No. I've been cooped up in a log cabin in the woods, with a bullet hole in my arm. I should have died, of course, but I didn't. Instead, I think I got the thug who tried to get me."

"Obviously, then, you are jumping at conclusions," said Mr. Burgundy, suavely. He was feeling quite at his best with the facts all against him.

"I heard Martin Field testify just now that Fortescue had murdered me. I heard that much as I came in. And I agree with the district attorney that he would never have thought of it if he hadn't himself planned it."

Martin here made a sign to his counsel and handed him a slip of paper. Mr. Burgundy read the note and pursed his lips doubtfully. After some hesitation he asked:

"Did you know that Martin Field had killed Fortescue? Were you, as District Attorney Mortimer intimated a minute ago, an eyewitness?"

"No."

"Then why do you think that the defendant wanted to kill you?"

Mr. Burgundy turned to find Martin holding out another slip of paper. He flushed as he read this, then shot a questioning glance at Martin. But Martin was very busy whispering to the assistant; sending him on some errand. So Mr. Burgundy sighed and put his question.

"Well, what about a white black bear? Does it by chance make any sense?"

"Of course."

"Will you please explain that paradoxical beast."

"Field telephoned me that he'd spotted an albino black bear up on his preserve and asked me if I'd like to go up and get him."

"He telephoned you?"

"Yes, at about half past five one afternoon. I was at the club. He was in a terrible hurry.".

"Yes, yes," quickly interrupted the lawyer. "He told you there was a spotted white black bear up at his place in the woods———"

"Not spotted—albino. He had spotted it."

"Never mind. And was there?"

"I don't know, but I doubt it. It was probably just a lure. He also said that there was a moose with an eighty-inch spread. I'm not sure there wasn't. But anyway, I was fool enough to jump at the chance.

"He gave me just time to grab my hat and meet him on the corner of Fifty-fifth Street and Sixth Avenue. I didn't see what his hurry was, but I wasn't surprised at the time—not after what had happened that afternoon at the club. I was there, you know. I'd sort of got him into it, is what he said.

"I knew he'd put himself in a damned awkward spot and didn't want to run any risk of being seen, but I never dreamed that he was sending me to my death so that he could kill Fortescue and then pin it on me. That's what he had this girl for.

"Given her time, she would have broken down and confessed that I was the one who really killed Fortescue because of her, though I've never laid eyes on her before. He made it so it would seem that I had run away and mysteriously disappeared. That's the first thing they told me at the flying field.

"Look what happened to me! It's only by the grace of God I mistook the thug for a deer and nipped him first."

At this Martin let out such a guffaw that the whole trial halted. And it was some seconds before Mr. Burgundy could proceed.

"You say he telephoned you at the club at five-thirty. You mean about five-thirty—not definitely——"

"Yes, definitely. Or to be exact it was five-thirty-two by his watch. I forgot what mine said, but I set it to his. He gave me exactly fifteen minutes to get to Fifty-fifth Street."

"Did the defendant say where he was telephoning from?"

"No."

"Did he meet you at—where was it?"

"Fifty-fifth Street and Sixth Avenue. His car was parked just east of the Avenue on the north side."

"He had probably just driven uptown from his office."

"Oh, but he wasn't in the car."

"Where was he then?"

"I had to wait for him about a minute and a half. He was walking; I saw him coming east from Broadway."

Mr. Burgundy smiled. "That would be in an opposite direction from his rooms, wouldn't it?"

"I suppose so. Yes."

"A very important point," said Mr. Burgundy, completely at a loss by this time. Turning to Martin for inspiration, the lawyer was exasperated to find him sitting back, thumbs in the armholes of his waistcoat, and that bored smile on his face which had characterized his earlier appearance in court. He waved an encouraging hand to his counsel, as much as to say, "You're doing fine. Go on."

Mr. Burgundy muttered "So" to himself and resumed the cross-examination. "Go on from there," he directed Van Leer.

"All right, I will," said Van Leer. "Well, he was in a hell of a hurry to get away. He said hardly a word, just hustled me into the car and rushed me toward New Jersey. He didn't attempt to explain what was up."

"Isn't that explainable, perhaps, by a natural reluctance to meet any of his club friends?" suggested Mr. Burgundy.

"That's just what I was saying. I thought it perfectly natural at the time. But I hadn't thought he'd be as jumpy as all that. He hardly spoke until we were halfway through the tunnel. Then he explained that he was sending me up by plane. Well, in that case there wasn't any hurry—except not to be seen.

"We took all the back streets. But I was so excited I didn't notice much. We talked about equipment. I was just as I had come from the club. He didn't give me time to leave any word where I was going. When I suggested it, he said he'd do it for me. The only thing that mattered much to me was a letter I was expecting from the State Department. My family are all abroad. It's easy to see he had figured that all out."

He paused and Mr. Burgundy looked to Martin before he muttered, "Go on."

"Well, there we were over in Jersey City. We pulled up suddenly at a dirty-looking little back-street drug store so that I could get some toilet articles. I got myself a toothbrush and a razor and a lot of chewing gum and some other things.

"There was a pawnshop a couple of doors from the drug store, and while I'd been buying those toilet things Martin had been looking at the things in the pawnshop window and he'd spotted a revolver that he thought would be nice for me to take along to pop at partridges with.

"I'm pretty good with a revolver, so I went in and bought it; then we went on toward the flying field. Only just about then Martin began to stall. He said there wasn't any hurry after all."

"One moment, please." Mr. Burgundy was being perfunctory. Things had, indeed, been growing steadily blacker for his client during Van Leer's recital. "That revolver, now?"

Van Leer started up as if something had occurred to him.

"Yes, that reminds me. It's nothing very important, but just indicative of how cold-blooded—— But I'll come to that. Well, we left the drug store and drove on through back streets. It was getting quite dark. We stopped once while Martin got out for some reason or other.

"Then we stopped at an old-time saloon. We had a drink and Martin decided that it wouldn't do to start before ten o'clock. He thought that it might be cold enough for the lake to have frozen and that would make it hard for Chuck, the pilot, to find open water to land if we got there before sunup.

"We stopped off for dinner at a dreadful place. It was as big as the Pennsylvania Station and we had it to ourselves. I guess we were both a little tight or I wouldn't have got up the nerve to have asked Martin about what he'd said at the club about choking Fortescue with that letter.

"At first he didn't seem to remember, which was just put on, of course. But then he laughed and said that if everybody took him as seriously as all that, he'd have to make good. Then he wanted to know about the revolver we had just bought. So I—— Here's how cold-blooded he was: he made me file a notch on it—a notch for Fortescue! Can you beat it? I thought he was just being funny."

"Yes, but one moment!" Mr. Burgundy looked despairingly at Martin, who only smiled back at him with that fatuous bravado which his counsel was beginning to find misplaced. Did not the notch on that revolver amount to a confession on Martin's part?

"Well, now, what kind of a revolver was it?"

"Colt .32."

"Colt .32?"

"Yes. Why?"

A funny feeling took Mr. Burgundy in the pit of his stomach.

"What did you do with it? Did you take it to the woods with you?"

"No. I had it in my coat pocket, and when I changed into Martin's flying togs I left my coat on the wing of the plane. That's the last I saw of it. Not having it nearly cost me my life."

The funny feeling in the pit of his stomach became a creepy feeling up and down Mr. Burgundy's spine. With a shaking hand he reached for Exhibit A.

"Was it a police revolver, like—like——"

"That's it," said Van Leer, without any hesitation.

Mr. Burgundy's mouth fell open. He dumbly placed the revolver in Van Leer's hands.

"Yes," insisted Van Leer positively, "there's the notch I filed for Fortescue, rest his soul. I wonder that Martin Field stopped short of making me file one for myself. I imagine he was quite capable of it."

Mr. Burgundy reeled a little, became faint. Dizzily he regarded Martin. That everlasting smirk! Did it mean—could it be possible —— Was it even remotely conceivable that Martin Field was going to get off?

Look at Field sitting there, having the time of his life! Mr. Burgundy had never felt so put upon. His one sustaining thought through all this despairing case had been that his client, smirk or no smirk, would eventually get what was coming to him.

But suppose he were innocent after all—all that beautiful evidence wasted—and that he, Felix Burgundy, had all this time been defending an innocent man! If this were actually the truth! The truth!

Burgundy fumbled for his handkerchief, dabbed his forehead, inhaled the reviving scent of Eau de Cologne.

In any life and death emergency like this, Mr. Burgundy would have thought, "My reputation first; women and children next." And so he forced upon his reeling senses a measure of self-control.

"Is this revolver the one you bought at the pawnshop in Jersey City, say, at something after six o'clock, and which remained in your possession till ten o'clock?"

"Yes. Why?"

"Why? Why, indeed! This is supposedly the revolver with which Creighton Fortescue was murdered—the one found beside the body. If Creighton Fortescue was murdered at five-thirty——"

"I object!" cried Mortimer, suddenly, bristling on the alert. "I object to the form of the question."

"In that case," said Mr. Burgundy with sarcasm, "I will let the district attorney ask his own questions. Your witness."

Mortimer stepped forward. "It's all a put-up job," he hurled at his adversary.

"You're telling me!" Mr. Burgundy hurled back with equal intensity. And something in the expletive sound that followed these words of simple dialect suggested the word "Fishy"!

CHAPTER 19

MARTIN REMEMBERS

"Yes," said the girl, "that's him. That's his voice."

THE prosecution was entirely unprepared for such a disclosure as this about the revolver. Secure, however, in an almost positive conviction of the prisoner's guilt—for there was the letter in the dead man's mouth, and all the rest of it—Mortimer assumed a contemptuous attitude.

"It was the State's intention to call this witness in rebuttal. It will, in the main, abide by that intention," he said. "But there is one question." He faced Van Leer. "Was the revolver loaded when you bought it?"

"It wasn't. But I bought some cartridges with it."

"Did you load the weapon?"

"No."

"Then you could not have fired it."

"I didn't."

"This revolver was found beside the body of Creighton Fortescue loaded. One chamber had been fired. You know that, don't you?"

"No; that's the first I've heard of it."

"Come, now, unless you want to be held as an accessory to this murder, tell me when this revolver was actually bought and so patently marked for identification? Where, to begin with, is this pawnshop?"

"I don't know. Somewhere in Jersey City."

"You're lying. There wasn't any pawnshop. The revolver belonged to Martin Field. He has terrified you into perjuring yourself in his defense, hasn't he? Or else he has bought you. Or, worse still, you let your admiration for him trick you into being his accomplice. Do you realize what perjury may mean for you in this case? It means that you make yourself his accomplice, that you will be held under the same charge of murder. A pawnshop two doors from a drug store. How long do you think it would take to disprove this testimony? You must have been well scared or pretty silly to let yourself get roped into this.

"Well, now is the last chance for you to save yourself. Don't be afraid of Martin Field. He'll never kill anything again. The police will give you all the protection you need. Now, out with the truth about that revolver. Where did Martin Field come by it?"

Van Leer had risen to his feet totteringly.

"You have called me a liar," he said, a pink spot glowing suddenly in each white cheek.

"Sit down, and answer my question," shouted the district attorney. "That sort of talk doesn't go here. This means business. Do you know what you are facing?"

"A dumb ass," replied Van Leer furiously.

Even the judge gasped.

But Van Leer went on. "Every word I said was gospel truth. Police protection? Phooey! That was what I came to you for. I'm trying to help you get the man who almost got me. And all you do is to call me a liar and set me up an accomplice. Ass!"

"Silence!" The sound of the gavel echoed through the courtroom.

Mortimer said nothing for nearly a minute. He appeared to be thinking hard. Then he smiled.

"The State will investigate this story. It will question this witness again in the rebuttal."

A number of court attendants now stepped forward to assist Van Leer from the chair. The poor boy was obviously very ill, and the effect of testifying had brought him near collapse.

Meanwhile Mr. Burgundy, completely bewildered, found himself confronting his assistant, who was guiding another young woman inside the rail. This one was not so good-looking as Gretchen Demarest and obviously she was not as young as she looked.

What was this the assistant was saying? The record of the telephone call—pay station on Broadway?

The assistant thrust the girl at him and immediately rushed off on further business quite beyond Mr. Burgundy's staggered comprehension. He could do nothing but what was indicated. He put the girl on the stand.

Her testimony was brief. She remembered a man of Martin Field's description coming into her telephone pay station on October 17th at between five-forty and five-forty-five p.m.

It was Saturday and she was all set for a date, if he'd only known it. (Martin Field's loss, of course.) This was substantiated by the record of a call, the club's number.

She also remembered the gentleman comparing his watch with her electric clock and saying she must be wrong, or else his watch was nearly ten minutes slow. He also said that he'd just come past the Pennsylvania Station. So she had called Meridian 7-1912, and he had remarked that he would be late for an appointment.

Martin was then asked to stand up to be identified. But she was not sure; she would know his voice, however. He repeated, "This will make me late for an appointment—except, of course, we compared watches. So he'll be late, too, won't he?"

"Yes, that's him. That's his voice. And that's exactly what he said."

"You testify that the defendant called this number, his club's number, at what would have been five-thirty or five-thirty-two by his watch, which was ten minutes slow?"

"Yeah, I guess it would have been just about that."

"Was he very drunk?"

"Drunk? No, he was as cold sober as a street hydrant, with a no-parking sign on it."

"Thank you." Burgundy bowed to Mortimer with exaggerated politeness this time. "Your witness."

This district attorney could only attempt to bully a confession out of the girl that she had known Martin Field previous to this encounter.

Failing in this, he contented himself with establishing the exact time of the call as being five-forty-two, which, being ten minutes after the murder, would have given the defendant ample time to have walked as far as the pay station. A clumsy attempt at alibi.

Suddenly Mortimer's entire case against Martin Field had wilted away. Martin had certainly not murdered Creighton Fortescue while drunk. Not unless the girl were lying, too.

But why wasn't she lying? She was probably another member

of the gang who had pulled this murder. She might have been
Van Leer's mistress.

Mortimer flung this at her and she denied it so hotly, but with
so much archness, with such an over-the-shoulder glance down an
open road, that he withdrew behind his dignity.

What was he to believe? There was the letter in Fortescue's
mouth, and there was Martin Field reeking drunk, and there
was the gun with the fingerprint and the exploded cartridge, and
all the rest of it. Van Leer and the girl were both lying. Or had
Martin Field hired yet another accomplice to impersonate him
in making this phone-call alibi?

Mortimer questioned the girl further on her identification and
was able to bring out that she vaguely remembered him as having
a small mustache.

Martin, hearing this, tore a piece of black leather from the
binding of one of Mr. Burgundy's law books and held it up under
his nose on the point of a pencil.

"That's him!" cried the girl. "I know him now."

Mortimer immediately released the witness. Whatever this
testimony proved, it did *not* prove an alibi. It seemed a very
clumsy attempt at one at best, with all that business of comparing
watches. There was no doubt now, however, that the whole case
had been skillfully rigged to trick him. What was that phrase of
Burgundy's? "As neatly laid out as a suit of clothes."

The room began to seem very warm to Mortimer. He felt a
sudden sensitiveness about looking Martin's way.

Now the defense was putting the prisoner back on the witness
stand. Some one in passing jolted Mortimer. Could it have been
Martin Field?

The district attorney heard the clerk rattling off the familiar
nonsense "Raise your right hand do you swear to speak the truth
the whole truth and nothing but the truth so help you God?" and
then Mr. Burgundy beginning:

"Well, now, you say it has all come back to you—that you
remember everything. Is that so?"

"I—I think so. I'd have to start at the beginning to see if it
would all connect up. One thing is certain, I didn't kill Fortescue."
Martin spoke seriously.

"You didn't kill Fortescue. You remember that, do you?"

"Oh, perfectly. I remember that I was horribly disappointed.
In fact, I still am. He was a beast. I meant to kill him—if only
to save myself. It would have been self-defense."

Mr. Burgundy took out his handkerchief and dabbed for forehead.

"When did all this come back to you?"

"I remembered it the instant I saw that girl—just like a tune I'd been trying all day to whistle."

"Are you referring to the young lady who testified that she had killed him?"

"Yes, Gretchen. I forget what her other name is. You see, we met under very exceptional circumstances. We each thought the other had done it. It was, in fact, pretty much the way she described it. I'd never laid eyes on her before that night when I got back from seeing Van Leer off to the woods."

"You were drunk, weren't you?"

"Not very. I remember, of course, all that Van Leer testified. That came back while he was telling it. And it's all just as he told it. We did have quite a few drinks, and we did buy that revolver. And it's true I was nervous, but not at the thought of meeting my club friends. I didn't want Fortescue to see me. He'd have put me on the spot.

"Well, we had dinner at that big barn of a place Van Leer described, and we filed a notch on the revolver. That was a grim joke. How did I know Fortescue was dead? But I meant to get him, because I had to get him before he got me.

"Well, Chuck yelled 'contact,' and I spun the propeller and off they flew. Then I saw the overcoat on the ground. I picked it up and went back to the car. There I saw the box of cartridges on the seat and thought about the revolver. I found it in the coat pocket. What was I to do—leave it where some kid might get hold of it? I just took it along.

"While driving back I got a hunch that I was walking into danger going to my apartment. Call it scared, if you want. Fortescue might have had Benny or one of that gang laying for me. So I stopped the car and loaded the revolver and—you know what junk you buy in pawnshops—I fired one shot through the floor of the car just to try it."

"So that explains the one exploded cartridge," interrupted Mr. Burgundy.

"I'm not trying at the moment to explain anything," replied Martin. "I'm just trying to remember what happened. You'll have to draw your own conclusions.

"Well, I went on home—but all that part is rather vague. I got home, anyhow, and up to my rooms. I remember that I was pretty nervous—on my guard. There's just one apartment on each landing, and I'm on the top.

"Well, I smelled perfume. A woman's scent. After two weeks in the woods, your nose gets very keen. That put me on my guard again. I smelled the glass doorknob and got it stronger. So I took out the revolver before I opened the door. There might have been a little sweet-scented gunman there waiting for me. But I knew he wouldn't shoot till he was sure it was me and not Fortescue.

"So I pulled down my hat, got inside and closed the door. It was pitch black. I gave a little whistle. I whispered, 'Benny!' But pretty soon I was satisfied there wasn't any one there. So I groped over to my big writing desk to turn on the desk lamp.

"I wasn't so sober, either, groping in the dark. I knocked over a silver polo trophy on the table—one I'd been using for an ash receiver—and I made a fearful mess. Then I switched on the light. Everything looked the same as usual. I hung up Fred's coat and my own. Then I went into the bathroom——

"Let me see. I'm forgetting again, where was I?"

"You are now in the bathroom."

"That's right. I must have washed up a bit. Oh, yes, I remember looking at myself in the mirror. You see, I'd grown a beard up in the woods, but I'd shaved all this off before I came back, all except a little mustache.

"I looked at it for a while in the bathroom mirror and decided the first thing I had to do was to shave it off. I didn't want people saying I was trying to disguise myself. So, off it came. Then I guess I went and got another drink.

"Yes, that's what I did, because I remember thinking that somebody had been at my liquor. I don't keep much. So I got it out to see if it was all there. And I found a little jar of caviar, too. I'd just washed my hands, so I used my finger for a spoon. Then I poured myself a small drink, lighted a cigarette, and started to sit down."

"At the moment of sitting down, how long was it from the time you had entered the apartment?"

"Oh, no, more than five or ten minutes. Only I didn't sit down. I had to clean up that mess of cigarette butts."

"You mean from the silver cup you had knocked over when you came in?"

"Yes. I picked them up—all thirty-six of them, if we can depend on the district attorney's accuracy. I put them in a real ash tray this time so that the chambermaid would throw them out. Then I took a swallow of the drink I'd poured."

CHAPTER 20

THE VERDICT

Mortimer smiled as he saw the cruel, even horrible way he could still win.

MARTIN was again rubbing his forehead. "Seems to me the next thing I remember, I was standing outside Fortescue's door with the revolver in my hand."

"You had heard a woman's cry, perhaps," suggested his lawyer. But Martin only stared blankly.

"Or did the girl come up and tell you she'd done it?"

"No, I know she didn't do that, because—because it doesn't fit. There I was taking a drink—wasn't I?"

"You don't remember going down two flights of stairs? You don't remember why you went down?"

"No. I can only remember standing there quite drunk, and then the door opening suddenly and—and there, almost in front of the door, Fortescue dead on the floor.

"I don't think I saw the girl who opened the door; not at first. It was dark, except for the light from the hall. Then, too, everything was going around crazily.

"I went in and kicked Fortescue—you know, to see if he was dead. He seemed to be stiff. I knelt down and felt him. He was

cold. I guess it was about that time I saw the girl. She was sort
of whirling around with everything else. I remember being mad
at her.

"What was it she said I said to her: 'This was my job. You
get out.' Well, that's probably what I said. And she said: 'Why
did you do it?' And I said: 'I meant to, only somebody beat me
to it.' And she said: 'Same here. I came here to do it. Who did?'
I told her I didn't know, but for her to get out and leave that little
nickel-plated gun behind.

"But she wouldn't go. She wanted me to go. She said I was
drunk and the police would get me. She said she had nothing to
live for, nowhere to go, and that it didn't matter about her.

"Then she told me Fortescue had said he was out to get me
and that she knew he would unless she got him first. And she
knew all about our stock deal, too, and what I said at the club,
so that unless she gave herself up now they'd be bound to get me
for it. Any one would naturally suspect me. She had been practically certain herself that I'd done it the moment she saw
Fortescue.

"Then she kept repeating that she had nothing to live for that
all she wanted was just to be near me for a few minutes before
they came and got her: that would be easier for her than jumping
off the bridge. And if it wasn't the one thing it'd have to be the
other, so there was no use in my getting mixed up in it.

"About that time everything began to whirl around and around.
I think I must have grabbed hold of her to keep her from
whirling about so, and I imagine she clung to me. That's when
I asked her to marry me—and she told me her name was Gretchen.
Then I said everything would be all right because I knew who
had killed Fortescue."

"Did you know that?"

"No, but I supposed Benny or one of his crowd did it. I told
her I would fix it up with the police, but I wanted her to keep out
of it. I got her into the hall and told her to go to the nearest drug
store and call up the police.

"After she'd gone I must have almost passed out. I had a
spasm of rage and went back and kicked Fortescue. I must have
gone pretty much off my bean. I remember taking the letter out
and making a ball of it and stuffing it in his mouth. Then I vaguely remember being back in my room and trying to pour myself
another drink. I guess that's where I passed out cold."

Mr. Burgundy interrupted. "That, I imagine, pretty well sums
up the case for the defense. And it leaves nothing unexplained—

not even the locked door. Have you anything more to say?"

Martin smiled. "Nothing, except that I should like to reaffirm that offer of marriage made while in an irresponsible state. No braver thing was ever done in the history of the world than what she did here to-day. I hope the State will not object to that being put in the record."

The district attorney's gardenia had wilted. His case had wilted and he, himself, had wilted. All his pertness and dapperness had gone. He was beaten. Incredible! All that *prima facie* evidence wilted, too!

Was it possible that Martin Field had framed the whole thing —even to the girls—bringing Gretchen Demarest in out of pure showmanship? Unbelievable!

It was certainly frightfully hot in the room.

Mortimer looked at the girl. How really pretty she was! She was gazing toward Martin where he still sat in the witness chair. Very slowly the district attorney turned toward Martin and saw the look in his eyes. Then he smiled and put up his hand to his wilted gardenia, for he saw one way in which he could still win. A cruel, even horrible way, but the only one that Martin had left him to get even. That is, if Martin forced him to use it. He smiled sadistically.

"So it all came back to you—this lost memory of yours. Convenient, wasn't it?"

But here he stopped. If Martin had, indeed, framed him, there was no point proving it, and perhaps the less said about it the better. Martin might gloat, but it would be in secret. Mortimer began again:

"I have no doubt you can account for your time between your arrival by plane from Canada and your telephone call to Mr. Van Leer from that pay station on Broadway?"

"Yes, I think so," replied Martin easily.

"And that shot you fired through the floor boards of your car——"

At this Mr. Burpundy's assistant, somewhat out of breath, stepped forward with the floor board and mat and a boy from the garage.

"I see," said Mortimer. "Yes, there is the bullet hole. Your Honor, in the light of this new evidence that has so dramatically been brought to bear on this case, I would like to ask a postponement of a few days."

The judge gazed sourly upon him over the rim of his desk.

"New evidence? The only new evidence has been adduced by the defense. Has the prosecution any new evidence?" He paused. "Unless the State is prepared to attack the testimony of Frederick Van Leer, I see no reason for holding up the trial and further inconveniencing the jury. The revolver that was offered in proof of Martin Field having killed the deceased is definitely not the weapon with which the murder was committed."

"Very true," admitted Mortimer. "But even crediting that testimony, and that of the telephone operator, no alibi has been established. The threat to kill Creighton Fortescue and the letter found crammed in his mouth, definitely connect Martin Field with the crime.

"Whether or not having killed him, he attempted this clumsy alibi of the telephone pay station, and whatever his real intentions with regard to Van Leer, and whether or not the evidence was framed, the State is adverse to relinquishing its charge against the prisoner and will still hold him for first-degree murder."

The judge nodded in thought. "The State then asks time to prepare a new case against the prisoner, does it not?"

"It asks time to substantiate new charges of a serious nature," replied Mortimer.

"Under such circumstances, I should be more inclined to throw the case out of court and ask you to find a new indictment of the prisoner," said the judge.

"Very well," replied Mortimer, and snapped his jaws shut.

Martin immediately stood up in the witness chair.

"I object."

The judge gave him, too, a withering look. But Mr. Burgundy sprang into the breach.

"The defense objects, Your Honor."

"State your objections."

"May it please the court, the defendant, an innocent man of the highest honor, has shown every possible respect for the law of the land. Being charged with this foul crime, and being totally unable to deny it—even believing, as I believed, the charges which had been brought against him—he refused to offer any defense.

"He said to me, his lawyer, 'If I did this thing I prefer to take the punishment.' That is nobility of character for you!

"Has he not already suffered sufficient humiliation and borne imprisonment long enough? The State asks that the case be thrown out of court so that the district attorney can put the prisoner back in a prison cell until a new indictment can be thought up.

"But the defense objects. It asks that the trial shall continue, that the case shall now go to the jury and the defendant be found guilty or not guilty of the charges against him. The defense rests."

"Objection sustained," said the judge. "I will, however, give the district attorney until three o'clock this afternoon."

The dark look on Mortimer's face deepened. He smiled.

"That would be of no value. Unless I can have two days as a minimum——"

"I see no occasion for allowing you this postponement," said the judge. "Unless you are prepared to indict all the witnesses for conspiracy and perjury."

Mortimer held his tongue. It was his life's bitterest moment.

"The prosecution, also, rests." he snapped. And turning briskly, went back to his table where he proceeded to gather and pack up his papers. He was through.

Martin rose from the witness chair with the faintest gesture of suppressing a yawn. And, nobody opposing him, he stepped down with that nonchalance which had given the trial so much tone in so short a time.

He gazed idly about the courtroom, ran his eye down the line of the jury, and turned slowly on his heel with his hands in his pockets, a vague expression of amused tedium on his thin, bronzed face.

Then he strolled to his seat and slowly sat down—and every woman in the courtroom sighed as he disappeared from view.

The judge looked at the clock. He spoke to Mr. Burgundy; he took note of Mortimer's departure. Then he addressed the jury.

"It is for the jury to find the prisoner guilty or not guilty of charge of having murdered Creighton Fortescue. I shall limit my instructions to informing you that it is now one-twenty-seven o'clock—long past the usual hour for the noon recess. I shall not waste time charging you as to your verdict. I shall hold the court in session while you retire."

The jury was out exactly three and three quarter minutes. The verdict was "Not guilty."

The judge immediately rose. Court was adjourned.

CHAPTER 21

ANOTHER VERDICT

Mr. Burgundy opened his eyes to such a sound of laughter as must have seemed to him inappropriate.

MARTIN was free. A man cannot be tried twice for the same crime, not even though he confess it openly. Such is the law. He leaped to his feet and seized the amazed Mr. Burgundy roughly by the arm.

"Get the letter—that Exhibit C!" Field yelled.

"I'm afraid——"

"Never mind that. I must have it!"

He got no further. The pent-up flood was upon him. Laughing, he fought free from reporters, autograph hunters, importunate females. He stood on a chair; he even climbed onto the table. There was no escape. Hands pulled at him, voices shouted questions at him, flashlights blinded him.

But Gretchen—where was that girl?

He held up his hand for silence, but in vain. He shouted and waved his arm over his head, pleading to be heard.

But the excitement was too great. The people in the halls were forcing their way into the crowded courtroom. Shouting, calling out to Martin, fighting for standing room, they pressed about him, hemming him in.

"Please! Officer! Burgundy! Let me out of here!"

A flash bulb blinded him. A young girl appeared on the table beside him and got both arms around his neck. But he ducked as graciously as circumstances permitted and knocked three reporters with cameras off the table. Then everybody began to yell at once, "Stand back!" and for a moment a vigorous counter-thrust of those about him gave Martin space to turn around.

Where was that girl? Where was Gretchen? And where the hell was Burgundy? He saw the clerk of the court pushing through a cluster of officials to a door behind the bench. Where was that letter?

A microphone was being held up in front of him.

"Would you mind saying a few words?"

Martin laughingly obliged with:

"A beautiful trial, wasn't it? I hope you all enjoyed it as much as I did. The D.A. certainly lived up to those initials, didn't he? If you know what I mean by that. Of course, I——"

But at this point he saw that by jumping to another table he could get into the jury box. The next moment he was saying, "Pardon me," to one of the lady jurors, as he stepped, not too delicately, from one seat to another directly across her. He vaulted a rail and got to the little back door.

But here was another jam of officials.

Some one had fainted. Martin heard the familiar cry for air and the inevitable cry of "Stand back," which everybody always shouts on such occasions and which nobody ever seems to apply to himself.

A sudden sickening fear possessed Martin. He was perfectly sure that it was the girl who had fainted.

"Gretchen!" he cried, and using his strength on three wispy-looking court stenographers, he forced his way through the ring. And there in the center of it, flat on his back staring at the ceiling, lay Mr. Burgundy!

The shock of seeing the recumbent lawyer sent Martin into an explosion of laughter. The circle about the prostrate attorney was startled, but presently responded, and Mr. Burgundy in due course opened his eyes to such a sound of laughter as must have seemed to him inappropriate, if not actually lacking in sympathy.

"Take it easy, old man," gasped Martin. "Have a glass of water. There now, miracles do happen in these unbiblical days, don't they? Did you get that letter? Why, so you did!" He took the crumpled sheet from the dazed Mr. Burgundy's relaxed

fingers. "Did any one here see where that girl went—the one
who confessed?"

"The State's holding her," some one volunteered.

Martin knit his brows. "Well, I'm glad of that, for one reason.
She can't run away. I know, at least, where she is. How are you
coming, Mr. Burgundy? Feeling better? See you later. Hi, officer!
How do I get to the warden's office?" And laughing as he thrust
through the crowd, "I suppose I ought to know my way by now."

"This way," said the policeman.

The warden was at lunch, but an official attached to the sheriff's
office attended to him, restoring to him the money and valuables
found in his pockets at the time of his arrest.

"Six hundred and forty-three dollars and and sixty-two cents
cash," said the official. "Your watch, keys, wallet, gold pencil,
cigarette case and lighter and nail file. There you are, sir. It's
a lot of money to be carrying on your person, if you value your
life."

"Never too highly. That doesn't pay, does it?" replied Martin
genially. "Have a cigarette. And tell me how do I get to—I mean
there's a young lady being held here. I want to see her at once."

"You will have to have a special permit."

"Get me one." And Martin detached a twenty-dollar bill from
the bundle of money he was about to return to his pocket.

The official's eager fingers recoiled at the touch of it. Martin
slid a second bill forward, but the man put both hands quickly
behind him and cleared his throat. Martin withdrew his offer.
He said in a low voice:

"Notify me at once at this address—you can leave word the
moment she is released. Keep her here if possible till I get here.
You know who I mean?"

The official nodded, but his expression was enigmatical.

"We'll keep her," he said.

"Where's the D.A.?"

"He left about a quarter of an hour ago."

Instinct told Martin where he would find his adversary. There
was no hesitation in his mind.

"Where's my hat and coat?"

"You didn't come here with a hat and coat."

"That's so. Well, thank you. Is this the way out?"

The man nodded.

A moment later, Martin found himself hatless and coatless in
the street. He hailed the first taxi; flinging himself into it, he
gave the driver his club's address.

Just why he knew Mortimer was there he could not have put definitely into words. But, obviously, if Mortimer were ever going to show his face in that assembly again, doubtless he would want to get there before he, Martin, did. He would not have wanted to face a laughing squad lined up to receive him.

No, he'd be there. He'd have had a chance to put on an attitude, to line up his own adherents. But that was not all. There was another reason. Martin felt that he was not done with Mortimer yet.

He took the crumpled letter from his pocket, the letter that Fortescue had written him, the letter with which he had sworn to choke Fortescue and which he had actually crammed into the dead man's mouth. A pretty trophy for framing.

Looking at it, Martin complimented himself on his own clever-ness. How quickly he had realized what the existence of that letter meant to Fortescue—a death warrant for Martin Field. Instinct again. Martin had acted quickly to save himself from being found obscurely murdered. It was certain death from which the police could have offered him no protection. He had simply killed Fortescue before Fortescue had killed him.

But at least he had given Fortescue fair warning. And he had not hired an assassin, but he had done it with his own hand. No one, not even the lawyer who had defended him, had been im-plicated in it; that is, no one was implicated by intention. Only the girl, Gretchen, had shared in it.

He rapped on the window and called the driver to stop at the first florist shop.

Murderer? Funny-sounding word—three syllables ending in R. But what did it mean? To have killed a man—not in war, nor yet on some lawless frontier, or on *safari* in the jungle, or on some honored dueling ground, or like the public prosecutor to have sent some innocent man to the electric chair by legal trickery.

Stigma? To offer your hand to a man who refused it. To have men turn their backs on you. Or even to know that such would be the case if they knew that your integrity was an imposture. Which was worse?

Murderer! Murderer! Murderer!

The taxi was drawing in at the curb. The florist's, of course. Martin leaped out and entered the fragrant shop.

"What flowers have you got?" he demanded. "Roses, freesia, carnations, these whatever they are and these, and these. Have you got a card? Thanks."

He wrote hastily, "Martin," put the card in its envelope, and addressed this to—he had to think—to Miss Demarest.

"Do you know where the city jail is? The Tombs prison? I want you to take these flowers to the warden's office. How much?"

Less than two minutes after getting out of the taxi he was back in it, rolling swiftly up Fifth Avenue.

As he got out and paid the driver at the club, two newsboys brandished extras at him. He shoved them off, pushed through the doors, and ran up the marble steps of the lobby.

"Hi, boys!"

The place was instantly in a ferment. There was a big representation of members present. They drew about him rapidly from all parts of the clubhouse.

"Hi, boys! Well, here we are! Pull up your electric chairs and sit down. Where's that wonderful district attorney of ours? Where are you, Mortimer, old man? Where is he? Hi, Peter! Quiet enough for almost anything to happen, isn't it? Reminds me of Sumatra.

"Why, if there isn't Van Leer. Hello, Freddy! Don't get up, boy. Sit still. He almost got you, too, didn't he? And if he had got you, I'd have gone to the chair. Did Chuck take good care of you? You'll never want to accept another invitation of mine, will you? But, of course, not. You won't have a chance. Got your appointment, didn't you? Hope it's the one you wanted. British East Africa—but if you'd rather have Sumatra I can fix that up for you, too.

"Hi, boys! He's in the dining room, is he? Oh, here he comes. Well, hurrah for crime! Waiter, champagne for everybody."

District Attorney Mortimer came into the room without speaking and stopped a few paces from the group about Martin. He stood there, facing them, his thumbs in his vest pockets, self-possessed, inimical, silent.

"Well, here you are," said Martin. "And here . . . . remember, gentlemen, the terms of our bargain that afternoon. It remains for our district attorney, to give him and . . . . . . to perform a slight office—that of framing and presenting, with a suitable address this letter to the club. Here it is, Mortimer, old man—Fortescue's letter."

Mortimer kept his thumbs in his vest pockets. He smiled.

"The terms of our bargain were that you would yourself kill Fortescue," he said acidly.

"Who says I didn't?"

"Ah, that's a different matter. If you are prepared to incriminate yourself—but I hardly think that you would go that far for the slight satisfaction my inconsequent office with regards to this letter could afford you."

"Why not, my dear fellow? Why not? I killed Fortescue. Now what are you going to do about it? A man cannot be tried twice for the same crime."

"Not, perhaps, in a court of law," replied Mortimer. "But then, you are not serious. You must realize what such an admission as this would mean. It would mean, for one thing, your immediate resignation from this club. As a butcher of wild animals you are, perhaps, honored here, but not as a common murderer."

"Oh, well, if you must back out of it on a technicality," said Martin, returning the letter to his pocket. "I think your flop in court to-day makes us about quits, doesn't it?"

"Does it?"

"Caviar shall have for me henceforth a new relish. But don't start me laughing again. That fishy fingerprint! Such a beautiful trial! How about it, boys? Did the district attorney do himself justice? Did he look his best with his gardenia and all?"

A burst of laughter was the response.

Mortimer stood there impassive. "Either you killed Fortescue, or you didn't kill him," he said in a level voice.

"Ah, but who need ever know as definitely as all that, my good man?" replied Martin.

"You may not be tried again for murder," said Mortimer. "But there's nothing to prevent me from holding you as a witness."

"Isn't there? And suppose it came out under your brilliant cross-examination that I'd planted all the evidence that old Burgundy kept saying had been laid out as neatly as a suit of clothes? Suppose it all became history for posterity to laugh at that I'd framed you? You'd look rather silly, wouldn't you?"

Mortimer did not reply to this. He stared at Martin with a look of such furious comprehension that nobody present could have failed to observe it.

"It might be fifty-fifty at that," he said at last, forcing a smile. "But I think I'd prefer my half to yours."

"Then, perhaps, it need never be known for sure," returned Martin. "Shall we have a glass of champagne on that? Did I, or did I not, murder Creighton Fortescue—and is or is not our district attorney as big a fool as he looked in court to-day? A mystery never to be solved!"

Laughter and cries of delight as the glasses were raised.

But Mortimer refused the glass that was held out to him.

"Very well, it need never be known," he said. "I do not say that I could not force the truth from you under cross-examination. And, of course, a direct voluntary statement from you is out of the question. It would be much too unpleasant for you. So, it will, perhaps, forever remain a mystery whether you are common gunman killer and whether I am as big a fool as you think I am—unless, of course, that girl of yours breaks under the third degree and lets us both down. That would be unfortunate."

"The third degree!" Martin dropped his glass. "Why, you filthy swine, if you touch a hair of her head, you'll be sorry. I knew you were holding her. You seem bent on making a still bigger ass of yourself, aren't you?"

Mortimer spoke slowly. "Of course, I'm holding her—she is self-convicted on her own testimony. She killed her lover. A fairly common occurrence among that class. We've got her now, and by the time the police are through with her——"

Martin leaped at him. "You beast! You're lying. You know damned well she had nothing to do with the murder. You can't hold her for it."

"Either she did it herself, or she knew too well that you had done it—which amounts to compounding a crime, besides perjuring herself. Unfortunately for her," he said, "some one must pay for the crime."

He turned on his heel.

But Martin seized him by the shoulder. "Look here, Mortimer, you'll free that girl at once or I'll put the whole damn thing in the papers, even down to our bet that you'd pull the switch yourself. What a swell story that would make—the district attorney doubles as the common hangman!"

Mortimer swung around in amazement.

"Yes, I killed him, and I'm free," cried Martin. "Free to fight for that girl, with my life and my honor—and your honor, too! Now get into that telephone booth and call up the warden and tell him to turn that girl loose at once, or I'll use the same phone to call up the papers. And what a story I'll give them! It's your choice."

Mortimer considered this in silence for some moments.

"To say that you killed him—murdered him—will be to let yourself in for a good deal more than you will let me in for. Besides, you will have to give me proof of your having done it—say, by writing a letter of resignation to this club. Yes, I think that I would accept that as sufficient grounds for believing you and for releasing your girl friend."

Martin's jaw worked. He stood clenching and unclenching his fists.

"You had better be quick about making up your mind if you want to spare her the unpleasantness incidental to telling us what she knows. I don't say she wouldn't go to the chair for you. It's quite up to you."

But curious things were happening in Martin's brain. The room had become intensely hot, with the sweltering heat of the jungle.

The light filtering through the Venetian blinds of the high windows was suddenly the sunlight of Africa through the close treetops of the forest. The circle of men became a ring of savages. Above them on the walls were the beasts of the jungle come to life.

Even the dapper Mortimer shed his dapperness and turned into a sleek black savage with filed teeth. Martin found himself measuring his adversary's ribs for a spear thrust.

Then suddenly it all faded and he was back in the club and he felt lost, out of his element.

"If you so much as lay your filthy hands on her I'll kill you," he said.

"I can't say how far things have proceeded by this time," replied Mortimer grimly.

Martin paused and closed his eyes for an instant. Then all his irresolution left him. He thrust through the ring about him to the nearest writing table.

"My resignation? Very well. Here you are, and there is the telephone."

Mortimer pursed his thin lips, nodded significantly and took up the telephone. A few words to the warden sufficed. He turned again to Martin.

"Now, if you'll hand me that resignation——"

"I left it on the table," said Martin. "But allow me to hand you this."

He thrust Fortescue's crumpled letter into Mortimer's outstretched hand.

It should have been Martin's big moment. It was. But he had only to look from Mortimer's face to the circle of faces about him to realize how much it had fallen amiss. The full glasses of wine, that had been raised a few moments before, were now being set down untasted. The ring of friends was breaking, moving back and away from him discreetly.

Something cried for utterance within Martin. Murderer——is

that what? Damned silly taboo! If I hadn't got him, he'd have got me. It was gunman and poisoned gin against straight shooting. At least I did my own killing, as a man should. But not one word of this passed his set lips.

Nobody, in fact, spoke till Mortimer broke the silence by calling a waiter to fetch Mr. Field's hat and coat.

"Mr. Field is leaving not to return—ever," he said. "I believe he has a coat in the coat room. He will probably not want it where he is going, but still we do not want it here, either." Then

"I think I prefer savages," said Martin, snatching his overcoat from the attendant.

"An odd preference, but I congratulate you on it," replied Mortimer.

Martin turned, smiling. "This will make a swell story when I get some one to write it," he said. "A bit fantastic, perhaps. More like a movie."

Putting on his hat and swinging his cane he went down the club steps and into exile with something in his step and something in the angle of his head and something in the look of contempt on his lean, bronzed face that every man who saw him that day for the last time secretly envied.

Gretchen was waiting in the warden's office when Martin got there—a small figure of woe huddled in a big chair. She did not look up till he came and stood before her, and then, seeing him, the blood rushed to her face and she put up her hands to cover it.

"You poor kid," he said. "Come, let's get out of here."

He took her gently by the shoulders, drew her to her feet and into the curve of his arm.

"Yes, we're getting out of this damned town—this jungle of hypocritical laws and taboos. We're going away from all this, for good and all. It will be better for you than suicide, at any rate. You'll like Africa, my sweet, and if there's anything of the missionary in you it won't take the savages long to convert you. Now, what about packing your duds and having some lunch and —and getting married?"

She shrank down against him. She wasn't crying. It was as if all the tears had been beaten out of her. She said shudderingly, "I told you that——"

"Yes, of course, my darling. It's new life for a life I've taken. That's fair enough, isn't it? Come now, let's put a smile on it."

She looked up at him with that look of hers—and smiled.

Her arms went around him as their lips met.

www.ingramcontent.com/pod-product-compliance
Lightning Source LLC
Chambersburg PA
CBHW020145180626
46810CB00004B/1746